The Rogu

Beau and the Lady Beast
Lily in Bloom

Morgan Ashbury

EROTIC ROMANCE

Siren Publishing, Inc.
www.SirenPublishing.com

A SIREN PUBLISHING BOOK
IMPRINT: Erotic Romance

THE ROGUE AND THE REBEL
Beau and the Lady Beast
Lily in Bloom
Copyright © 2008 by Morgan Ashbury
ISBN-10: 1-60601-008-5
ISBN-13: 978-1-60601-008-2

First Printing, April 2008

Cover design by Jinger Heaston
All cover art and logo copyright © 2008 by Siren Publishing, Inc.

Printed in the U.S.A.

PUBLISHER
Siren Publishing, Inc.
www.SirenPublishing.com

Dedication

Beau and the Lady Beast
To my critique partner, Raina Toomey. Damn, girl, you're good.

Lily in Bloom
With great admiration and genuine affection to Diana DeBalko, who made everything possible by saying 'yes'.

Morgan Ashbury

SIREN ADULT FAIRY TALE

Beau and the Lady Beast

Morgan Ashbury

Beau and the Lady Beast

A Siren Adult Fairy Tale

MORGAN ASHBURY
Copyright © 2008

Chapter 1

"You want me to *what?*"

Beau Brannigan took a moment to appreciate the sight of Isadora MacLean in full temper. Living up to her reputation for having a beastly disposition, she'd surged to her feet, her breath heaving in a way that showcased her lovely silk-covered breasts.

Her scowl told him she'd noticed him ogling her chest. He flashed her a grin and answered, "Become my hostage for the next three days. It's a small enough price to pay for fifteen percent of your company. Let's see…going with the most conservative estimates, fifteen percent of twenty million dollars is three million. Divide that by seventy-two hours, and that's damn near forty-two thousand dollars an hour."

"That's absurd!"

Beau watched the shock wash through her and waited while she slowly lowered herself onto her chair. He wasn't going to point out this deal could effectively make her the most expensive courtesan of all time.

She'd certainly looked stunned when he revealed he'd purchased the stocks from one of her largest single shareholders. He understood the step she'd taken more than a decade before with her ISO had been, in her mind, a necessary evil. He also knew that ever since, she'd been buying up shares when they became available. Some had referred to the process as the *Lady Beast's Holy Grail*. The fifteen percent he'd just waved under her nose represented one hell of a big chunk of her company. Vital to her and valuable to him only because it gave him what he'd craved for the last year—the chance to get his hands on Isadora. It didn't matter, her being a dozen years older than he. He wanted her, and by damn, he was going to have her.

"Are you out of your mind? You want me to give you seventy-two hours of my time? To do what?"

"It isn't your time so much I want. It's *you*. And to do, Isadora, whatever it is I tell you to do."

Beau's plan was risky, that was certain. He understood her well enough to know she'd be suspicious of any overt attempt on his part to court her. Better to keep her off balance by way an indecent proposal. When she was in his home, when he'd spent some time with her, would be soon enough to reveal his heart. He smiled. Sliding forward slightly on his chair, he put his elbows on her desk.

"Tomorrow at noon, my car and driver will arrive at your home. You'll be driven to my country estate, about an hour outside of town. Once inside the gates of my property, you will become a voluntary hostage, completely subservient to my every whim. Oh, and you don't need to pack a bag."

"You want me to come to your home in the country for the weekend and not pack anything? Not bring a change of clothes? That's totally ridiculous. You're not making any sense at all."

"Of course I am. *If* I require you to wear any clothes while you're my guest, I'll provide them."

He could tell by the look on her face she finally understood what he wanted.

"You…me…you…*if* I wear clothes? You want me to be *naked*?"

"In my experience, having sex is easier if the parties involved are naked."

"Sex. You and me. Are you crazy? You think I'm going to have sex with you?"

"In exchange for fifteen percent of your company? Yes, I think you will. You look a little piqued, darling. Why don't I make you some tea?"

She was, he mused, a woman who obviously liked to have her creature comforts at her fingertips. A tiny service area took up one corner of her office. Beau blessed all those years spent in front of a camera when he'd been dubbed the most beautiful man alive. The skills he'd acquired then allowed him to affect a relaxed pose. She wouldn't see his nerves. He could hear the sound of her sputtering, but not her actual words.

Using the hot water dispenser, it took only moments to make a cup of tea and set it before her. He resumed his seat, and his bravado.

"You want me to sell my body to you in exchange for those stocks. You want to turn me into a...a...whore? Are you out of your ever-loving mind?"

Her choler captivated him. Red slashes of fury decorated her cheeks and icy darts shot from her electric blue eyes. Her voice rivaled the thunder and he wondered why her assistant hadn't come running in response. She was, quite simply, the most stunning creature he had ever seen. He could admit that, and the fact that he likely needed therapy.

"Don't look at it that way. It's not my intention to make you feel like a whore."

"Then I don't understand. Is this...some sort of payback, or something? Did I do something to piss you off? Seizing the opportunity to cage the *Lady Beast* and humiliate her? Humiliate *me*?"

"Is it so hard for you to understand that I simply want you? You're a beautiful woman. This has nothing to do with payback or humiliation, and everything to do with pleasure. You're not currently in a relationship, are you?"

"No."

"Then there really is no reason why you can't give yourself to me for the weekend, is there?"

"You can't be serious. You're going to...to...*for seventy-two hours?*"

Beau chuckled. Her temper had cooled as quickly as it had fired. Now, her face had gone pale, and she seemed to be having trouble putting sentences together. Her eyes had dilated and her nipples hardened. Two signs, he hoped, of arousal and not just extreme shock. He wanted to hug her and assure her all would be well, but he needed to maintain the role of roué. "I may allow you some time to eat. To sleep. Shall we make a small contract, just between the two of us? You have a printer here, which is handy. Two copies, and we'll both sign them. From noon tomorrow until noon Monday, you will be a willing hostage to my every whim. I'll absolutely guarantee your safety, but not necessarily your comfort. In return, upon completion of your, shall we say, 'personal service', I will sign over to you the stock in MacLean Cosmetics I've so recently purchased. Or you can say no, and I keep the stock. I'm sure you're aware fifteen percent is enough of a base for a canny manipulator to engineer a hostile takeover. I can be exceedingly canny, when the situation calls for it. The choice is entirely up to you."

In all the rumors about Isadora he'd heard, there'd been no talk of a personal life. She lived, slept, and breathed her company. She'd earned the nickname *Lady Beast of Bond Street* because her office was her lair from which she guarded her empire ruthlessly. Beau believed that the tough exterior of the Lady Beast hid a warm and compassionate woman, and if he had her to himself, even if just for three days, he could set that woman free.

But he had to get his hands on her first.

Beau tramped down the arousal that began to grow when she licked her dry lips. He noted the fine quiver in her hand when she picked up her tea and sipped.

"I've never…what you're asking is that I give up all control. I've never *not* been in control. Never thought I would ever be."

"Nervous?"

"Very."

"Good. I can offer you a safe word. We could include in the contract between us that I won't hurt you. But then, once you're my hostage, I can do what I like, can't I? You'll just have to trust me. If you say yes." He sat back and let his eyes roam her body, much like he planned to let his hands roam as soon as he had her under his roof. "Can you do that? Can you trust me, put yourself into my hands? Do you accept my proposal?"

He watched the emotions play over her face and felt his heart surge in triumph when he saw her answer before she spoke it.

"Yes. I, ah, accept."

"Let's get it written up then, darling. One copy for me, and one you can place wherever you like, for safekeeping."

* * * *

Isadora hadn't expected a chauffeur-driven limousine. Settling herself into the back seat, cut off from the driver by a glass partition, she wondered if she had finally lost her mind. The moment the chauffeur closed the car door, she began to tremble. She wasn't certain if she felt terrified, furious, or excited.

The bizarre agreement had been written up, signed, and a copy locked in her desk drawer before she'd allowed herself time to reconsider. Now, of course, it was a matter of honor.

She was stunned that Beau Brannigan could really want *her*. Black hair and green eyes, with the kind of sinfully sexy good looks that had sold millions of dollars of whatever merchandise he'd been hired to model, Beau could easily have any woman at all. She recalled the first time she'd set eyes on him, in person. He had absolutely taken her breath away, and when he'd smiled at her, she'd felt the clutch of sexual attraction deep in her belly. The arousal had shamed her, even as it had intrigued, for he was nearly a dozen years younger than she. She'd done her best to ignore the sizzle, but as the months passed, and she came to know him, she wondered about the sense of connection she felt, and wondered if it was reciprocated. If it could *be* reciprocated. Then she'd remember the years between them. She'd very nearly convinced herself that her attraction and growing feelings for him were completely inappropriate.

Truthfully, her sex life had been nothing to brag about. She understood—intellectually, at least—that part of the reason for that was how badly her one and only waltz down the matrimonial aisle had burned her. It might be unfair to paint every man she'd dated with the same brush as Neil MacLean. But that was life.

Her cell phone rang, pulling her out of her memories.

"Yes?"

"Tyler here, Isadora. Just stopped by the office to see you and your assistant said you were going away for the weekend."

Disbelief laced the voice of oldest friend and lawyer, Tyler Parkinson.

"What, I can't take a weekend off?" Isadora smiled, looking out the window of the limo at the passing scenery.

"Well, you haven't for a long time, Dory."

"I'm entitled to have a life after all these years of hard work and no play. But then, I believe I already mentioned my intention to change things." She couldn't keep the laughter from her voice, and could easily picture her old friend's scowl.

"Please don't remind me. It was that sentiment that led to your completely irrational and foolhardy decision which had me tromping all over the city earlier this week."

"You're a good friend, and a good lawyer, Tyler. Thank you for doing what I asked you to do, even when you didn't agree with it."

"That little piece of business made me feel like neither. I really don't think you covered your ass very well. Have you had any response yet?"

Tyler sounded so aggrieved, she wanted to laugh. If only he knew.

"Some," she wanted to change the subject before he got too curious. "Was there something in particular you needed to see me about?"

"No, just wanted to drop off copies of the injunction I filed on your behalf yesterday."

"No problems?" she asked. The small matter of an unfaithful employee had prompted her to get Tyler working on another front.

"No. All straight forward. Theft is theft. I left the copies of the court papers with Charlene."

"Excellent. Thank you, Tyler."

"You're welcome. So, where are you going for the weekend?"

Looking around, she could see only trees and fields. "The country," she replied.

"You? In the country? What the hell are you going to do there?"

"I think I'm going to get my feet wet. I'll see you next week, Tyler."

Not giving him a chance to respond, she hung up. Then, considering, she turned off the phone before she tossed it back in her purse.

Sitting back, she let her mind travel over her meeting with Beau, and her current situation. Something he had said—or intimated—flooded her thoughts. He wanted her completely under his command. Control wasn't something she'd surrendered to any man, ever.

She wondered what he was going to do when she declined to surrender it to him.

Chapter 2

Isadora perked up when the car paused at the entrance to a gated country lane. The gate swung open slowly, and she had to suppress a nervous laugh. The car eased through, and she turned, the sight of the gates swinging closed again knotting her stomach. Trees canopied the long and winding lane. The brush was so thick on either side, she could see nothing beyond a few feet. Then the lane curved sharply to the left. Before her, a stone-and-glass building, immense, seemed to stretch to the sky.

Far from the 'country home' of a well-to-do corporate executive she'd imagined, this was more like a magical castle from the heart of a fairy tale. It lacked only a moat. Then the car stopped, and the driver opened her door. Thirteen steps led up to the massive wooden door. Ascending, she counted them and chided herself for being foolish. Beau Brannigan was a flesh-and-blood twenty-first century man, not some spellbound recluse from the pages of a fairy tale. Despite his choice of words, she would certainly be no hostage, voluntary or otherwise, but a businesswoman visiting an associate for a weekend in the country, to cement a business deal. There, that felt a lot more calming and reassuring.

It was an illusion she held onto until the door opened.

* * * *

Beau hadn't been entirely certain she would come. Until the moment when he knew the limousine had driven onto his land, he'd hoped, but hadn't been sure.

He opened the door abruptly, catching her off guard, and watched with admiration while she got herself under control.

"Isadora. I've waited a long time to have you in my home. Please, come in."

"Your home is unexpected," she said, turning her head this way and that to look around.

Beau smiled when she faced him.

"The expected would be boring, wouldn't it? Actually, this is a forty-room reconstructed castle. My grandfather, who had more money and whimsy than sense, brought it over, stone by stone, from England several decades ago."

"That must have cost a fortune and been logistically complicated."

Beau laughed out loud and then impulsively hugged her. It didn't matter that she was a bit stiff in his arms. He needed the contact right then and there.

"Grandfather didn't care. If he set his mind to something he wanted, he let nothing—certainly nothing inconsequential like cost or logic—get in his way. In this, my pet, I take after him."

"I'm not your pet, Beau."

He'd anticipated that response. "My darling, this weekend, and starting right now, you're whatever I choose to make you."

He cupped her face, caressed her lip with his thumb. His heart beat just a bit faster when he saw her eyes widen, when he understood that, just so simply, he'd aroused her. Carefully, he dipped his free hand into his pocket to take out his first surprise. In an instant, he had it secured exactly where he wanted it. Quick, unforeseen, and over before Isadora could even have guessed what he intended.

He watched her reach up, her fingers touching the jewel-encrusted leather collar now encircling her neck.

From his other pocket, he withdrew a leash. One quick flick attached it to the collar.

"See? You wear my collar and my leash. So you must be my pet. Ah, ah," he added when mutiny clouded her face, "you did agree. *My every whim.* Considering the liberties I'm about to take with your lovely body, a collar and leash are small things."

"Bastard."

"Remember our deal. Behave…and submit." He enjoyed watching her struggle to get her temper under control.

Finally, she lowered her hand.

"That's better."

"It's only for seventy-two hours, after all." Her words emerged from between clenched teeth.

"Ah, but what fun we can have in seventy-two hours." He took a moment to look at her body, making his stare lascivious. "I've a pot of tea waiting in the front parlor. Just to show you how magnanimous I can be, pet, I'll let you drink from a cup instead of lapping from a saucer."

The room he indicated was just to the left of the entrance hall, across from the stairs. Taking the first few steps, he noticed Isadora standing her ground. The color in her cheeks was high, and he bit back a smile. That saucer comment had been spontaneous and obviously a direct hit. He judged the distance. One more step, and the leash went taut.

"Did I misjudge your integrity, Isadora?" Unable to resist, he punctuated his question with a small tug on the leash.

Her hands clenched and unclenched, and he could almost hear her mentally counting to ten.

"No one questions my integrity."

He could have relented, let the leash go slack, but he wanted her to submit. For a long moment, she held his gaze, and defiance filled her eyes. Then, without the tiniest sign of giving way, she walked toward him.

"This can be a pleasant interlude, or a nasty one. It's entirely up to you," he said, careful to make his tone amiable, his voice soft.

"You said this had nothing to do with humiliation." The edge in her voice was more than temper. If he hadn't made such a point of paying attention to her during their many encounters over the last year, he would have missed the hurt.

"It's not my intention to humiliate you, pet. I'm just trying to demonstrate the parameters of what's expected of you. Don't think of it as humiliation, and it won't be. Think of it as…training."

Temper fully eclipsed the hurt in her eyes, and he smiled, satisfied. He'd much rather have her mad than pained. "Come, our tea will get cold."

He saw her seated on the love seat, casually draping the leash over the arm of it. Then he served her tea and set a plate of cookies on the low table before her.

"It's Earl Grey," he said, sitting across from her.

"My favorite."

"Yes, I saw that in your office yesterday. I hope you didn't have any trouble getting away?"

"I had no plans to change."

He wanted to know how that could be, but he didn't ask. Instead, he enjoyed his tea and watching her. Interesting that she looked everywhere but at him. When she did finally meet his gaze, he grinned.

"I don't know what I'm supposed to do." Genuine confusion laced the words.

"And in any given situation, you always know what to do."

"Yes."

"Because you're always the boss."

"Yes."

He wondered if she'd heard that grudging tone in her voice. He was touched by the sadness she seemed to always carry with her. Usually, she kept it more deeply buried. He'd hoped this weekend might bring it, and much more, to the fore.

"Always being the boss carries with it a burden of responsibility. I know you meet that responsibility head-on. But everyone needs a break, pet. This weekend is yours. You don't have to be responsible. You don't have to worry. Just be co-operative, that's all I require. Are you finished with your tea?"

"Yes, thank you."

"I'll show you to your room, shall I?"

He used his hand at the base of her spine to guide her so that she walked beside him, rather than employing the leash. He escorted her up the stairs and then turned right, stopping at the first door on the right.

"Here's your room. Mine is just next door. You can rest and have a nice long bath, if you like, and yes, before you ask, you'll have complete privacy behind this door. Since you're bound to obey my every command, I don't need to stoop to voyeurism to see you naked. Dinner will be at six, sharp. I'll come and escort you." He opened the door, then unsnapped the leash. "Oh, and darling? Leave the collar on. I don't want to have to punish you so soon into our time together. Your garment for the evening is hanging on the armoire."

He had to give her a small nudge to get her to move into the room. Then he pulled the door closed and locked it.

* * * *

Isadora froze, the sound of the second "click" echoing off the walls. A lick of fear, instinctive and female, shivered down her spine when she realized he'd locked the door. She waited a moment, unsure, and then tested the handle. The test turned into a furious, vigorous assault.

The door remained stubbornly closed.

Her hand went up to the collar. It felt as if it had been made for her, sitting comfortably around her neck. She reached back to unfasten it. Panic fueled her fingers searching for the clasp.

There was none.

Her eyes scanned the room. Bars on the window and a locked door. Good thing she understood she wasn't *really* a prisoner.

A single garment hung on the outside of an antique armoire. The ivory silk robe, long and beautiful, begged for her touch. It boasted no buttons, zippers or Velcro, just a silk sash. A folded piece of paper stuck out of one of the pockets. She pulled it out, opened it, and read.

The deep V neck of this gown should show your collar off to perfection. As it is made of the finest silk, I'm looking forward to seeing how this robe caresses your breasts, ass, and thighs. Wear this for dinner, tonight, my darling Isadora. The robe, the collar, and nothing else.

Reaching forward, Isadora caressed the robe with fingers that weren't quite steady. She wondered how it could be that locked in, wearing a symbol of a man's control, she felt seduced.

Chapter 3

Beau had to restrain himself from taking her on the spot.

She'd put her hair up so that curls tumbled half down. The effect—the long, white column of her neck adorned by his collar, unhampered by red tresses—was very arousing. The silk caressed her sensuously. He'd known it would. Held closed only by the belt, he imagined reaching forward, giving one tug.

The game he'd chosen to play was proving to be hell.

"You're beautiful, Isadora."

"Thank you. So are you, but then, I've always thought you wore a tux very well."

He couldn't resist chuckling. "And you're feeling underdressed?"

"Maybe just a little."

"Well then, perhaps I can offer one more item." He held up the end of the leash, his thumb resting on the catch, and waited to see what she would do. He watched her eyes focus on the shiny metal, and he wondered at the emotions chasing across her face. She shuddered slightly, just once, and tilted her head, giving him free access to the small ring dangling from the leather.

"Good girl," he said softly. Unable to resist, he stroked his hand over her shoulder and down her back, finishing with a gentle caress across her bottom. His touch not only fed his arousal, it told him she wore nothing under the gown but flesh.

"That was very clever of you, demanding I not remove the collar, knowing I'd need a key to do so."

He didn't mind the bite in her words. He simply smiled at her. "You're an intelligent woman. I half expected you to have picked the lock."

"I thought about it. I very nearly did."

"What stopped you?" he asked, escorting her down the stairs.

"The realization that I *did* sign a contract. In essence, giving you my word. I'll have you know I've never reneged on a contract in my entire life. Well, except for that marriage one, but that was years ago and hardly counts."

Beau stopped at the bottom of the stairs and turned to her. "Was that all? Your honor? My promise of punishment didn't factor into your decision at all?"

Her face reddened slightly, but she looked him dead in the eye when she answered. "No."

"Liar."

He ran his fingers up and down the leash, then casually caressed her collar. "When the time comes, I'm going to enjoy taking you. I'm very much going to enjoy hearing you scream my name when you come." He leaned toward her and filled his lungs with the scent of her. "Lilacs. I see you availed yourself of the Jacuzzi. I trust everything in your room met with your approval?"

"How could they not? My favorites, every one."

His eyes drew to her nipples, beaded and poking out under the silk. "Yes, they were." Turning, he led her down the hall to the dining room.

He'd had the long table set for just the two of them, with a place setting at each end. The food had already been brought in, kept warm with silver domes and warming trays.

He saw her seated, then taking up the open and waiting wine bottle, poured her a glass. "I hope you enjoy the meal." He couldn't resist a light caress of her cheek. This kind of touch he knew he'd lavish on her constantly, and he wanted her to get used to it. Though she looked startled at the tiny familiarity, she didn't jerk back or jump. She blushed, and that delighted him.

"It smells wonderful."

He treasured her surprised smile when she lifted the cover to her plate. He'd had his housekeeper grill the fresh Pacific Salmon with a honey garlic glaze. The rice pilaf and fresh green beans also numbered among her favorites. He'd chosen a nice, crisp Chablis to accompany the main course of their meal.

"You're at my table, wearing only the robe I've allowed you and the symbol of my possession I've bestowed upon you. You've pleased me, pet."

He enjoyed the confusion that crossed her face. Time to switch gears.

"I hear you've had a brush with corporate espionage recently." He watched her mentally follow the segue and wondered what she thought about as she nibbled so delicately on her food.

"My V.P. in charge of advertising thought she could cut a better deal by taking herself—and the ad campaign she'd designed for MacLean—to a competitor."

"I hope you skinned her greedy ass."

"Well, it's a clear case of theft. My lawyer has initiated proceedings. Poor Mary Ellen doesn't really know who she's messing with. The little bitch."

Beau smiled when she stabbed a fork full of beans for emphasis. "Good for you. You can't let people get away with theft—whether it's product or ideas."

"Don't worry, I don't."

"Neither do I. Tell me about your ex-husband."

She stopped her fork halfway to her mouth. "Why?"

Shifting gears was a good strategy. "Because I want to know."

"Not much to tell. I made a mistake. I never repeat them."

He didn't mind the acid in her tone. After all, it wasn't him she was remembering with such venom. "There must have been something good about him to attract you in the first place."

"It happened a long time ago."

He simply waited, his head cocked slightly to one side.

"I was so impossibly young," she said softly after a moment. "Looking back, I find it hard to believe I ever could have been so young. I'd just started my company, with an inheritance from my grandmother. I approached each promotional opportunity with the enthusiasm only the young can manage, and at one of the functions— a concert, I think—I met Neil. I didn't know at the time that he'd been watching me for a couple of months. That I was at the top of his 'list.' I didn't know he planned on courting me, marrying me, and then cleaning me out, financially, that he'd done just that to at least two other women before me. I only saw what he let me see. He appeared cultured, smooth, and seemed to be infatuated with me, and I fell for it. I fell for him."

Beau didn't like the sadness in her voice. She'd stopped eating and seemed far away. He knew better than to offer her pity, though. There was only one way to pull her out of her funk. He needed to rile her.

"You annoy me, Isadora. How can you still blame yourself for the dishonesty of another, after all these years?"

Her eyes focused on him with a fierce scowl. "Well pardon me all the way to hell and back. The bastard betrayed me. Not just with his dick, which doesn't strike me now as being a particularly memorable one. He took my money, my self-respect, and broke my heart. At the time I loved the asshole. So excuse me for *hating* that I fell for him."

Pissed was better than vulnerable in his opinion. "And he wasn't worth even one of your tears, sweetheart. I bet he's still looking for marks, and it burns his ass to know how well you've thrived without him."

The look on her face spoke volumes. He wondered how she'd managed to cut herself off from people so completely that simple words of support floored her.

"Whenever I think of him, I feel stupid."

He rewarded her candor with a gentle smile. "And you haven't let anyone get really close to you since." He heard the gentleness in his own voice and hoped she did, too.

"No."

"Until me."

He waited patiently, the silence between them lengthening. He waited and felt his heart kick once, hard, at her whispered response.

"Until you."

Chapter 4

She'd never been more churned up and confused in her life.

The echo of the door being locked still reverberated in her head. The taste of Beau's kiss, their one and *only* kiss, still clung to her lips.

After dinner, he'd led her into the library, a wonderful room filled with books and the rich scent of leather. A fire burned in the hearth, and the gentle warmth of it filled the room. By the fireplace, a chessboard had been set up, and once she was seated, he brought her an after-dinner liqueur. That it was her favorite, peach schnapps, didn't surprise her in the least. It appeared he'd done his homework, and she truly didn't have any secrets from Beau Brannigan. Settled comfortably in the chair, her drink at hand and the game underway, Beau threw her off balance yet again.

"Isadora, open your robe. I want to look at you."

She hadn't consciously decided to grant his request, but her hands reached for the belt and untied it. Then, when he just sat there with that maddeningly sweet smile on his face, her hands had gone that one step further, folding back the fabric, baring herself to him.

"Very nice. You have beautiful breasts, pet. Yes, and your nipples stand out quite a bit when you're aroused. Good. The nipple clamps will work well. They're silver, in the shape of small rings. If you like the look of them, I'll consider making the look permanent. Two rings, one in each nipple. Perhaps with a tiny silver chain on each, running from the rings to the center of your collar. Would you like that, pet?"

She wanted to scream no, of course she wouldn't! Picturing what he described, she felt arousal stir in her belly and moisture gather between her thighs. She couldn't hide her reaction or bluff it off, either. Somehow, he'd known.

"I'm glad that turns you on. I bet there are a lot of things that will turn you on. I'm going to enjoy discovering each and every one. It's your move."

Not in their personal tango, she knew, but in the chess game. "How do you expect me to be able to concentrate when I'm naked before you, and you're looking at me like that?" When you have me so horny, she meant. She couldn't say it, but she couldn't hide it, either. He knew.

"By relying on your competitive streak."

He pushed his chair back from the table just slightly. Unplanned, her eyes moved to the very obvious erection tenting his trousers.

"If I can do it, then, pet, so can you."

She couldn't seem to remember the difference between a rook and knight. Before she was ready for it, the game, and the evening ended. Nearly midnight, he escorted her to her room. She'd felt the air caressing her breasts, her belly, and her mons as she walked with the silk robe gaping open. The shivers coursing down her back came from more than the cool breeze.

At her door, he turned her. And he kissed her. He touched only her face, cupping it between his hands, his thumbs tracing an invisible pattern over her cheeks. His touch gentle, as if she were precious. His mouth avid to sample and taste. She couldn't stop herself from responding. No, that was a lie. She hadn't even thought to refuse him. His tongue stroked hers in a strong, almost forceful rhythm, touching and tasting every part of her mouth in a single instant. All she could do was hold onto his wrists with her hands and return the kiss. How often had she wondered what it would be like to have his mouth on hers? Reality outshone imagination. She could taste the brandy he'd had while she'd sipped her schnapps. She could taste him, his flavor more intoxicating than any alcoholic drink could ever be. On and on the kiss went, and she nearly stumbled when he pulled back slightly.

"You'll be awakened at seven. We'll have breakfast at eight."

It had taken her long seconds to understand that this kiss wasn't a beginning, but an end. Before she could comment, he'd opened the door, unclasped the leash.

"If I'd wanted just a quick lay, you can bet I'd have had you flat on you back with you legs spread before now. So think about that, pet. Oh, and sleep naked tonight, Isadora, wearing only my symbol of possession. Sleep naked, and dream about all the delicious things I'm going to do to you tomorrow."

Now, standing alone in the center of the bedroom, she shook her head slowly. Sleep? How was she supposed to get to sleep when every inch of her felt painfully wired? She looked around the room and felt her face heat when she saw the bed had been turned down. An envelope rested on her pillow. Beau hadn't left her, which meant he had staff in the house.

She'd walked through the place with her assets hanging out, and he had staff in the house!

"At least he put it in an envelope," she muttered, picking up the thing and pulling out the folded single sheet within.

Your clothing is being laundered. In the armoire is your outfit for the morning. After you've been awakened, shower and dress. By then, your door will be unlocked. Join me in the dining room.

Curious, Isadora opened the armoire. The storage space held but two pieces of clothing: a pair of white slacks and a matching white tee shirt, both of summer-weight cotton. If they fit, they would be snug, and very nearly transparent. Then she realized there truly were only two items in the closet. A quick search of the room revealed what she'd suspected. No underwear of any description could be found.

She never slept naked. Just one of those things she'd never done. But Beau had asked her…no. Isadora closed her eyes, inhaled deeply. He hadn't asked her anything. He'd *ordered* her to sleep naked. Before that, he'd called her his pet, and *ordered* her to bare herself to his sight.

Thoughtful, she got to her feet and approached the wooden closet. She slowly removed the robe and hung it up, then slid into the bed. Turning off the light, she lay in the dark and wondered why being commanded by Beau had felt so right, and why obeying him had become the only thing she really wanted to do.

* * * *

"It's beautiful."

"I think so, too." He'd brought her outside for a walk on his land, and now they overlooked his favorite place, on the banks of a large pond. "This piece of property belonged to the farm my great-great-grandfather established when he came from Ireland in the eighteen hundreds."

"No longer being farmed?"

"Well, I have a few acres devoted to corn and hay. But no, for the most part, the Brannigans moved from rural environs to the city in my father's childhood. But I've always loved it here."

"It's so quiet. I've been a city dweller all my life. I grew up in an apartment, never even lived in a house until just after I started my business."

She fell silent, and Beau knew her thoughts had turned back to less pleasant memories. Stepping behind her, he wrapped his arms around her, cradling her against his chest. He couldn't help but speak from his heart. His respect for her had always been huge, and his love for her was growing. He wondered when she would recognize the feelings he had for her.

"Now you have a beautiful home in the middle of the most exclusive area in the city. You've furnished it with the best of everything from all over the world, and you did it all through your own brains and vision and guts. Your company is one of the most solid, most respected cosmetics companies in North America. This, too, is the fruit of your hard work, planning, and determination. That's a hell of a lot to be proud of, love. The rest that came before? Maybe you had to go through that to get where you are. To be *who* you are now. I happen to have very fond feelings for who you are now."

Beau closed his eyes in pleasure when she folded her arms over his.

"Thank you. That's...that's the nicest thing anyone has ever said to me."

"You're welcome." He resisted the urge to cup her breasts, to slip his hands under her shirt and pinch her pretty pink nipples into erection. It was absolute hell, being this close and not having, but he wanted her for more than a quick tumble. He could have her body now. He knew he could turn her in his arms, pull the clothes from her, lay her down, and plunge. But all he would have would be her body, and he'd decided, even before he'd brought her to his home, he wanted much more than sex. The time he'd spent with her so far only reinforced his determination.

Reluctantly, he released her and stepped away. "Come, pet. We've not finished our walk." He tugged on the leash and smiled when she didn't bitch or tug back. She blinked once, as if just now remembering the collar and leash. She tilted her head and looked at him, her expression serious.

"As you wish."

"Now you're getting it," he couldn't resist saying.

Chapter 5

"You want to play another game?" They were back in the library, but the chessboard wasn't set up.

"I do. Please, pick a seat."

Looking at the Scrabble board, Isadora shook her head. She could remember playing it as a child. The thought came out of nowhere that some things endured.

She'd brought her after-lunch tea with her and sipped it while Beau set the game up. He handed her a large pile of tiles.

"I thought I was supposed to pick them blindly, a few at a time," she commented idly, turning the letters over and arranging them.

"My board, my rules, and I get to go first."

"You like being in control."

"I do, but I know when to let go, pet. Never fear. Ah, here's an excellent first word."

Isadora knew her eyes widened when he laid four letters on the board. F-U-C-K, never a word she'd used for points before.

"I thought profanity against the rules."

"Like I said, my board, my rules."

Isadora found herself returning his smile, though she was sure hers wasn't as heart-melting as his. Examining her letters, she picked a single one, an "S," and put it at the end of his word.

"Ooh, you went for simplicity, I see. Let me just tell you what I think of that."

She watched avidly while he picked up four tiles and used her already placed "S" for another letter. She laughed. He'd spelled the word 'pussy'.

"I think you have a one-track mind. At least, when it comes to words. Aren't you going to keep score?"

"Who says I'm not?"

Shaking her head, she picked up two letters and placed them after the "P", adding the innocuous word 'pan' to the mix.

Quick with his next contribution, he placed an "S" at the beginning and a "K" at the end of her word.

"Spank. Is that a threat?"

"I don't make threats, only promises."

"Beau Brannigan, you're a very confusing man," she said, studying the board and her letters.

"I don't know what you're talking about. I'm an open book."

She shot a look of disbelief. Deciding two could play the same game, she used his "K" for the last letter of her word.

"Cock," he said, smiling. "That's more like it."

Too engrossed with enjoying his playful expression, she didn't immediately notice the word he formed next. He had gone back to the original two words and added four more letters.

"Fuckslave. Is that even a word?" she asked, and could have cursed when the slight tremor entered her voice.

"You'll be in a better position to answer that question, personally, after dinner. Your turn."

His remark had been without that bantering tone she'd come to enjoy. The expression in his eyes told her he was quite serious.

Over the last twenty-four hours, he'd pulled more out of her than anyone before. Enough that she spoke without thinking. "You keep me off-balance. I came here prepared for what I believed would to happen. I thought we'd have a few laughs, maybe…and a lot of sex."

"And I invited you here to share intimacy. Tell me, Isadora, have you ever been so intimate with another man?"

Isadora couldn't lie. "No." She couldn't pretend not to understand what he'd been doing to her, systematically, since she arrived. Looking down at her letters, she scooped up five and lined them down under the "A" in his last word.

"I know you're afraid. You don't have to spell it out for me."

She laughed, loud and sudden in the silence of the library. She felt an extra bond form between them when he smiled and winked at her. She watched him place one more word on the board, beginning with an "S" that fit onto a word already there.

"I win."

She read the new words: fuckslaves submit. Becoming aware anew of the collar around her neck and the leash attached to it, she understood in that moment he spoke nothing but the truth.

* * * *

She hadn't heard the lock turn or the door open. That was her first thought when she awoke and saw the box.

Plain white and decorated with a red ribbon, it waited at the foot of the bed and hadn't been there when she'd drifted off for an afternoon nap.

After their word game, Beau announced he would return her to her room so she could have that nap.

"I never nap in the middle of the day."

"You will today, because I order it. I want you fresh for tonight."

That had certainly been imperious of him, and she let him know it by the frosty look she sent him. She'd felt quite proud of that tiny rebellion, all things considered.

And hadn't she just ruined it all by being sound asleep when he'd made his delivery?

Tossing the blankets aside, she got to her feet and stretched. The second time she'd crawled into bed naked, she'd done so this time, automatically. She felt a bit more at ease with the concept, but not with standing awake, totally nude. She opened the armoire, unsurprised to find the outfit she'd worn that morning gone, but very grateful the silk robe still hung in place.

Feeling more secure with the robe on and belted around her, she approached the box. There was, of course, a brief hand-written note attached:

Your attire for the evening. I'll collect you at seven.

It took her a few moments after opening the box to understand what she was looking at.

"Oh, you have got to be kidding!" She pulled each item out one at a time, examined it carefully, set it aside. She removed six items in total from the box. When she had them on the bed, she arranged them, as they would be worn, and she picked up the item that had been at the very bottom of the container.

If she put *those* on, she'd be…what? Giving in to Beau Bannister's prurient fantasies? Well, *duh*, she'd done that the moment she'd accepted his proposition. No, if she put on this last item, she'd be telling him he really was in control. That she submitted to him and his self-proclaimed right to dominate her.

And what had giving up that precious commodity netted her so far? Isadora licked suddenly dry lips. The answer came to her with no effort at all. She'd never felt more pampered, more cherished, or more *special* in her entire life. She'd certainly never been so intimate with a man—hell, with anyone—as she had been with Beau. Before this weekend, she'd believed herself infatuated with the man, and curious if that infatuation could become something more. Now she knew she was falling in love with him, and here she stood, on the very precipice of crossing into totally unknown territory.

Could she continue being submissive? So far, it had been simple and, she acknowledged, superficial. Tonight, when he opened her door, if she wore everything he'd provided for her, it would go far beyond the superficial.

Tonight, if she wore this outfit, the real submission would begin. Her hand went to her stomach. It felt like she'd swallowed an entire hive of bees. She had no idea what plans Beau had in store for her. She felt a little bit afraid and a whole lot nervous.

The only question was, did she trust him—and herself—enough to do obey him?

* * * *

He unlocked the door and knocked.

She'd been his "guest" for just thirty hours. It seemed longer, somehow. Forever—that's how long he'd been waiting for her. Waiting for her to come into his life and into his bed.

Tonight, he was taking them just one step deeper into intimacy, and closer to his ultimate goal. He hoped. It all depended on what he saw when she opened the door.

The door swung inward, and his breath caught.

"My God, woman, you're hot."

"Thank you."

Touched that her cheeks turned pink, Beau couldn't resist reaching out to stroke them lightly. Neither could he resist continuing the caress down her body. The bra he'd chosen for her, French cut and siren red, displayed the top of her breasts and nipples. With his fingers brushing her flesh, nipples already pebbled poked out even more. His gaze swept down, noting with approval she wore the thong panty over the garter belt. She'd understood he intended to remove the one, but not the other. At least, not right away. The stockings and shoes showcased her long, sexy legs.

He'd left looking at the best for last.

The felt-lined black restraints he'd included with the ensemble encased her wrists. Ordinary handcuffs made of metal invariably connected the wrists together. He'd chosen these ones not only to match the collar, but for their versatility. He could restrain her with her wrists together, or her arms spread wide. Also, like the collar, these could only be opened with a key. He'd included no key in the box.

"I didn't know how you wanted me to wear them. I snapped them together, figuring if you didn't want them that way, you'd change them."

"You've pleased me, pet. Are they comfortable?"

"Yes."

Beau cupped her face, his thumbs stroking either side of her mouth. "Take that last step, Isadora. You've come so far already, and you're safe. You know that. Take that one last step for me, pet, and answer me again."

He felt the slight tremble and smiled when she lowered her eyes.

"Yes, they're comfortable. Master."

"Good girl." He kissed her, his tongue thirsty to drink from her, his lips firm and demanding. The taste of her, honey and ambrosia, shot straight to his groin. He felt her surrender in the tilting of her neck, in the widening of her lips. He pulled her tight against him so she could feel the strength of his erection. He used one hand, pressing on her ass, and was rewarded with the feel of her pussy grinding against his cock. He loved her, and at this moment he knew his goal within reach. Wanting her more than he'd ever wanted a woman, stepping back was hell.

He broke the kiss, smiling in response to the dazed and passionate haze in her eyes. He stepped back and handed her the clasp-end of the leash. She didn't hesitate, but attached it to her collar in one move.

"My grandfather wanted this castle to be identical to an actual medieval castle. He included a few features the rest of the family thought over the top. I've been a negligent host in not giving you the complete tour. So tonight, I make amends. First, we'll have a small snack in the dining room. Then, I believe we'll take our party to the dungeon."

Chapter 6

The dungeon was real.

One wall held what appeared to be medieval weapons. Daggers and swords, a mace, a large club, and a shield decorated the old stone. At the base of the weapon display stood a table, with a wheel at one end.

Isadora tilted her head and realized, with some shock, the table was a rack. A small cage, mid-room, hung suspended above the floor by a heavy chain.

She couldn't suppress the shaking that had begun when she stepped into this room.

"Now you understand why I only fed you a light snack. Are you afraid, my pet?"

And he had fed her, Isadora acknowledged. She'd sat on a low stool beside him in the dining room. He'd unhooked her handcuffs, fastening them behind her back. He fed her, one small mouthful at a time, from his own plate. He allowed her a few small sips from his wine glass. He even dabbed her lips delicately with a napkin, and then he brought her here.

Was she afraid? Isadora examined the emotions swirling within her.

"No, Master. I'm...nervous. And excited."

"None of these tools have been used. They're all replicas, for decoration only. But over here," he put his hands on her shoulders and turned her to face the other direction, "is where we're going to play."

Chains hung from the ceiling and wall. A black leather medical exam-type table, complete with stirrups, waited innocuously in the corner. A shelf held various items, some of which she couldn't identify. Those she recognized included a riding crop, a flail, a paddle, and a strap.

"None of these have been used before, either, but we won't be able to say that after tonight, will we, pet?"

"N...no, Master."

Her belly jittered when he disconnected her handcuffs from each other and massaged her arms.

"Sore?"

She didn't think she could speak, so she just shook her head. Her arms weren't sore, even though they'd been manacled behind her back for nearly a half hour.

"Hold your hands out in front of you so I can attach these chains."

A part of her wondered why the hell she obeyed his every command, calling him "master"—that tiny part of her that was a stubborn, foot-stomping shrew. And yet the rest of her, fascinated, wondered *what would come next?*

When he'd attached both chains, one to each cuff, he stepped behind her. She heard the rattle of metal, and then her arms, lifted by the chains, rose above her head, and away from each other.

"There."

Stretched to the maximum, her feet still touched the floor. Barely. She tested her bounds and found she couldn't lower her arms one bit.

"Rest your eyes now, pet."

The blindfold was soft, and he had it in place before she could take a breath. She felt him fastening it, the way one would fasten a watchband or a belt. It fit snugly, and she could see nothing. Blind and immobilized, she waited, totally at Beau's mercy.

She felt his body press against her back and she gasped for his hands came around her, touching her everywhere. It wasn't until she felt him cup her naked breasts she realized he'd unfastened the bra.

"I've wanted my hands on you for so long. I would see you across the room at cocktail parties and imagine you here, naked, mine to take. I would be trading snappy repartees with you at those functions and dream of the day I would have you hot and needy, writhing under me. Wanting only me."

Heat washed through her, and she could only moan in response. Her head fell back, and she heard his chuckle, low and deep, felt it roll through her belly. She was completely seduced, and if only he knew it, completely his already. Despite her nervousness, despite the situation, she knew she could trust Beau Brannigan, as she had trusted no other man. Completely and absolutely.

"You like having your breasts played with? They're luscious. Plump and ripe…and mine. How do they taste?"

He stole her breath when he moved around and suckled her. His hands stroked her ass and up and down her back. He used teeth and tongue and lips on one breast, then the other. His movements varied in speed, slow at first, then, unexpected, he'd feed ravenously. Unable to see, suspended, she felt disoriented, and emotionally off-balance. Sometimes breath-soft, other times sharp, almost painful, he doled out delicious torture.

"Please." She couldn't stop the plea, which came from her soul.

He moved his mouth up her body, then settled on her lips in a totally carnal kiss. She wanted to give everything and take even more. Her tongue met his, stroked and danced and tasted. Her arousal blossomed in the pit of her stomach, spreading out in all directions. Her hips moved convulsively, and she cried out when he moved himself out of their reach.

"Yes, you like your tits sucked. Let's see how you like this."

Isadora heard movement, something sliding, and then something soft and gentle caressed her. Whatever it was floated softly back and forth across her breasts, making her nipples pucker even more.

"The strands of this flail are velvet. Gentle, but they aren't always."

She heard him step back, and a whistle in the air. She nearly shrieked when the lashes of the flail streaked across her breasts. It hurt, but only a little. She clenched the lips of her pussy when it struck her again, and then a third time. She couldn't believe how the light pain increased her arousal. A fine electric current seemed to run from the strands of the flail through her entire body. She couldn't hold back the moan of pleasure.

Beau laughed softly, cupped her breasts, and placed gentle kisses on each. "A bit pink, but no real marks," he whispered, just before he suckled her some more. "And you liked it. I can tell. Let's see if you like this, too."

He stepped away, and she heard a tiny bell-like clang. Then, she sensed him step close, felt his cool breath on her still-damp nipple. The bud puckered even tighter.

The metal felt cold against her hot flesh. Two pieces, on either side of her nipple. She whimpered when the metal tightened, pinched, and knew these were the nipple clamps he'd spoken of.

"Can you take a bit more?"

"Mm…yes, Master." What previously secret nerve ran from the end of her nipples to her pussy? She was so hot, so wet. Moving her hips, she gave herself over to the sweet, stinging arousal that this man stirred in her.

"There, that's tight enough for the first time. Now, we'll do the other one."

Tiny, desperate mewing sounds echoed off the stone walls of the small room. *Was that needy, begging sound coming from her?* She didn't care. She just cared about, needed more.

The sound and feel of fabric tearing preceded the wonderful sensation of his hand brushing against her slit.

"I bought them, I can ruin them. Oh, baby, you are so wet for me."

"Please." She didn't care if she begged. She wanted more, and she wanted it now. Her hips moved, helping her pussy follow his hand.

And the stinging smack of something hard and flat on her ass made her jerk in shock.

"How many, pet? How many times should I spank your ass with this paddle?"

He struck her again, and the smarting pain, accompanied by the brush of his fingers against her mound, brought more arousal than she'd ever known, certainly more than she believed she could bear.

"Don't come," he ordered, his voice hard.

Don't come? She wanted to come so badly. Only a few minutes, and already, she wanted to come.

Her thoughts scattered, then focused. That's what sex had always been for her—get hot, get off. Wham, bam, no fuss, no muss. And no importance, really.

As if he read her mind, his next words cut to the very heart of her. "That's right. You want to come, but I'm not going to let you. It's only Saturday night. We have until noon Monday. I'm not going to be fast and clean and over. I'm going to be long and messy and enduring. I'm going to *matter*."

Oh, God. You already matter, more than I ever thought anyone could. But she couldn't tell him that, not when every nerve ending in her body was crying for orgasm.

"Now…how many more times shall I spank you, pet? Ten more?"

She cried out when yet another blow stung her ass. She could feel the flesh of her bottom getting hot and tight. She never would have imagined being spanked could turn her on like this.

"Yes, yes. *Please!*"

His tongue swirled in her ear, one hand stroking the lips of her pussy, back and forth, and the paddle fell in hard, fast slaps. Never the same place twice, unpredictable, the blows covered every inch of her ass. The pressure on her nipples added to the fire burning deeply within her. The sounds coming from her throat as she felt her wetness on his hand turned almost feral. She hadn't counted, but knew the spanking finished when she heard the paddle drop to the floor.

"Kiss me, sweetheart."

She needed to kiss him more than she needed to take her next breath. He hadn't just stimulated her body, he'd stimulated her heart. Opening her mouth, she devoured him. Such heat, such hunger ran through her it was a wonder she didn't melt. Barely aware her hands had been freed, she wound her arms around him. He was everything she'd ever wanted, everything she'd ever needed, and she had to have more. She'd die if she didn't get more.

She closed her eyes for a moment in the harsh light when he took off the blindfold. He kissed her lightly, then stepped back. He had the clamps off her nipples in mere seconds. The sudden cessation of stimulation made her feel almost drunk, certainly bereft, and oddly uncertain.

She hadn't even seen the lush velvet robe he bundled her into. When he gathered her into a hug, she clung hard and fast.

"Come on, sweetheart. Let's go upstairs."

Yes! Upstairs, where the beds were. Horny enough to take him now, she'd prefer a bed. She wanted Beau more than she'd wanted any man in a long, long time—probably ever.

She blinked in bewildered confusion when he opened her door, unsnapped the leash, and stepped back.

"I don't understand."

He bent down and kissed her, his lips and tongue both gentle. He tasted good, and she wanted more. Trying to take more, she tried to wind her arms around him, but he gently set her away from him.

"Inside, you'll find your clothes, the key to the collar and cuffs, and a notarized letter, dated today, confirming the terms of our agreement have been met, and that the shares in MacLean will be turned over to you Monday at noon. When you awaken in the morning, your door will be unlocked. Downstairs, there'll be a car with the keys in it. You can go home, if that's what you want to do. Or, you can come next door to my room. And we'll make love. Tomorrow. Your choice."

"I...I really don't understand. What was that downstairs? Just...playing?" She felt her temper climbing and didn't care. Damn this man all to hell and back, he really messed with her head! Not to mention what he'd just done to her body. No man set her on fire like that and then just walked away!

"No, darling. *That* was foreplay."

"It worked!"

"For me, too."

She felt some satisfaction when he grabbed her hand and pressed it against his engorged cock. She obviously wasn't the only one in need.

"But I need you to choose me when you're not high on arousal, when you're not flooded by submissive urges to please your master. I need us both to be certain that if we make love, it's because we have both chosen to."

He kissed her lightly, just once more. Then closed the door in her face.

Chapter 7

Everything was exactly as he said it would be.

Isadora stood at the window, looking down at the late-model sedan parked by the base of the steps. Her clothes had been returned to her, cleaned and pressed and ready to wear. She held in her hand the document Beau had mentioned. Those stocks were hers.

She could walk, and she knew instinctively that Beau, the next time she met him at a party or business function, would be charming, and witty as he'd always been. He wasn't a man to hold a woman's choices against her. There wasn't a petty bone in his body.

Pity she couldn't say the same about herself. She could be small-minded and mean-spirited when pissed. She had a temper second to none. Despite the fact that being called *The Lady Beast* sometimes hurt her heart, she knew she'd earned that name down to the ground and would likely continue to be more than worthy of it.

She should go back to the city and chalk the entire weekend up to temporary insanity.

The sun broke from behind the clouds, sparkling like diamonds on the stone and glass house. The green of the forest shimmered, as a soft breeze caressed the leaves.

Temporary insanity, her mind echoed, while her finger reached down to stroke the collar that lay on the dresser.

* * * *

Beau wanted coffee, but he couldn't bring himself to move away from the window to go get it. He knew she'd awakened. He'd heard her shower come on.

He wondered if leaving her high and dry last night had been the wisest course. Sure, he felt noble, if frustrated, but what if she made the wrong choice today?

He could court her. Flowers, candy, whatever it took to convince her she belonged with him—to him. Or he could make her his hostage for real. Refuse to unchain her until she vowed to spend the rest of her life with him. Until she accepted his love, and gave hers in return.

Fuck this. The waiting was driving him nuts. He'd waited long enough. The time had come to claim what belonged to him.

He spun away from the window and froze.

He hadn't heard the door open, but it had, of course, opened and closed. Isadora stood with her back against it. She wore his collar, and nothing else.

* * * *

"You didn't leave."

"I nearly did. I thought of all the reasons why I should just go. There were a lot of them." Isadora amazed herself. She didn't feel self-conscious standing naked before him. Now with the pretense of master and slave gone, there was nothing to figuratively hide behind any more. She had chosen to be here, her pride stripped as bare as her body.

"What reasons?"

She wished he'd come closer, rather than lean against the window frame. She shot a quick look around the room. The massive bed showed definite signs of a restless night. It was the only sign she had that he felt as she did, and she clung to it stoically as she answered him.

"To begin with, I'm too old to be thinking about changing my life, taking on a man for the long haul. My business eats up a lot of my time. I've gotten rather used to doing things my own way and not having to think about pleasing anyone but myself."

"Those sound like some pretty solid reasons for you to go."

"Hm. That's only some of them, but only one reason I could think of to stay." If he didn't do something soon, she was going to scream.

"And that reason would be?"

Finally, he took a step toward her. "Because I want you. It doesn't matter if it doesn't make sense, if people laugh behind my back because I'm so much older than you are. Nothing matters but being with you. You've already touched me as no one has. You *get* me as no one has. Damn it, man, put your hands on me!"

He could move fast when he wanted to. He scooped her up and brought her to the bed.

"I'm going to put my hands, my mouth, and my cock all over you, pet."

"Less talking. More action."

"Yes, ma'am."

She'd known. Somehow, she'd known that it would be like this. Even through his clothes she could feel the heat and the strength of him, and that heat and strength warmed not only her flesh, but her soul. Fast, hot, give and take. She tore at his clothes, greedy for the feel of his flesh under her hands. He seemed to be just as greedy for her if the speed with which he feasted was any indication. She had his shirt open in a heartbeat. He was beautiful, his chest broad and firm, dusted in brown hair. Then her mouth fastened on a male nipple, biting, licking, sucking. He tasted of salt and sin, musk and man. His was a taste she wanted never to do without again.

A hard hand cupped the back of her head, fingers tangling in her hair, guiding her closer. "More, baby. Give me more. Take more."

Her mouth explored his chest, then found his lips as three hands—one of hers and two of his—worked frantically to free him of his pants. She crawled on top of him before he got them all the way down his legs. And cried out when he lifted her off and set her on her back again.

"Beau!"

"In a minute, baby. I want to feel you. Let me."

She knew she drenched his fingers when they so easily slipped into her. She was so hot, so ready, that his hand was nowhere near enough. She wanted his cock, and she wanted it now. She felt him reaching into the bedside table drawer even as he fastened his mouth on her right nipple, nipping it sharply, then sucking the swollen bud into his mouth.

She loved the feel of his mouth at her breast, but it wasn't what she needed most right now. Pulling away, she said, "Give me the damn thing." Ripping the condom packet from his fingers, she had it open and on him in a heartbeat. Then, using all her strength, she pushed his back to the mattress and mounted him.

His cock, long and thick, slid inside her and she groaned. This is what she'd been missing all her life. He was what she'd been missing, and to have him now, a part of her, filled her soul with joy. Her pussy, hungry for him, took every last inch, squeezing tight, then releasing, and doing it all over again. He felt hard and slick and *wonderful*. He completed her.

Beau sucked in a sharp breath, his fingers digging into her hips. "That's it. Fuck me, baby."

"You feel so good inside me. Mm, yes, I need more."

"More?" he asked.

He was incredibly strong to be able to wrap his arms around her, lift them both, and change positions without taking his penis out of her.

"More, then."

He spread her legs wide, and she felt the muscles in them straining. He shifted his position and…oh lord, he pushed so much deeper now, moving harder and faster so that he hit her cervix. It hurt, but the pain just rolled itself into the arousal, taking her higher and higher. She could feel the flesh of his shoulders and back straining, and ran her hands over the hot silk-covered muscles, her fingers drinking of the feel of him. A fine sheen of sweat glistened his skin. Leaning up, she tasted his salt, the flavor of his sweat going straight to her sex. The scent of him, all man, swelled her senses until she thought she might explode.

"Yes, yes, keep taking me, pet. More."

His voice, no longer smooth, no longer velvet, conveyed his tension. The animal in him emerged, and Isadora loved it. She tilted her pelvis, wrapped her arms around him, and added fuel to his fire.

"Fuck me harder, master! Fuck me harder." Her orgasm gathered as he did exactly that. The sound of labored breathing, of his balls slapping against her flesh echoed in the room. Primal sounds, they tore away the pretense of civilization.

"Now, sweetheart. Come on my cock now. Come with me now"

"Beau!" She screamed his name, her orgasm exploding through her. Wave after wave of pure rapture convulsed her pussy and rippled from her belly to her fingertips. She wrapped herself around him and held him, just held him through the convulsions of his own orgasm, absorbing the energy, the emotion and the intimacy. On and on it went until, finally, drained and replete, she fell back on the bed. Beau collapsed on top of her, and she wanted him to never leave her.

* * * *

"I knew it," he panted. "I knew it would be beyond good with you. Shit, lady, I think you wrecked me."

Her laughter was music to his ears. He managed to roll to his side, bringing her with him, tucking her close.

"I love you, Isadora. I love you."

"I think I figured that out when I kept finding my favorite things all over the place, but mostly when you went to so much trouble to show me I didn't have to worry that a relationship with you would hurt me."

"I knew you were smart enough to figure that out." He held her closer, nuzzling her neck. "I like the way you taste, right here."

"I like the way you taste, too. Everywhere."

"You haven't tasted me everywhere yet," he teased, and laughed in delight when she blushed.

"I will."

"Good. I've been gone over you since the first moment I laid eyes on you, more than a year ago. I kept trying to get you to see me as a man, one who wanted you, but you wouldn't."

"Oh, I saw you all right. You turned me on, more than I'd ever been turned on in my life, but I thought myself foolish. An older woman in mid-life crisis lusting after a young stud."

Beau couldn't help it. He laughed and hugged her tighter so she'd know he wasn't really laughing at her.

"Sweetheart, you're only forty-two, not sixty-two. You're too young for a mid-life crisis." More seriously, he stroked her face. "I'm going to be forever grateful to Cyrus Carmichael for deciding to sell his stock in your company. It was perfect timing, and the perfect lure. I knew that if I could just get you alone …what?" Her face colored in a light blush, and her eyes skittered away from his. Intrigued, he scooped her up and laid her on top of him.

"About that stock. It wasn't Cyrus' idea to sell it to you. It wasn't even his stock. It was mine."

"Yours? I don't understand. I got a call…"

"From Max Kessler, who said he'd been speaking to Cyrus, who wanted to sell his fifteen percent in MacLean. My lawyer arranged it all, at my request. Gave me grief over it too. He called me irrational and complained I didn't cover my ass."

"I like your ass uncovered. But why, sweetheart? Fifteen percent is a pretty hefty chunk. Why did you want me to buy it?"

"Because I wanted a *life*. I wanted something more than just my business. I had it all planned out. You'd buy the stock, then take an interest in the company, come to meetings, and get involved, and then I'd find a way to get you to make a move on me."

Beau felt his smile spread. "Yeah?"

"Yeah."

He watched her fingers play with his chest hair. He could feel his erection growing, and knew they wouldn't be talking for much longer. "When I came to your office, you seemed so shocked."

"I *was* shocked. You moved a lot faster than I dreamed you would. What you suggested was way over the top. I thought."

"The reality of it turned you on, though." He couldn't get enough of the feel of her under his hands. He stroked her, back to thighs, lingering on her ass.

"Yeah. Enough to suggest that we take this party to the dungeon later."

"Later. You know I want you to be my sub only when it comes to this, don't you?"

"I figured that one out, too."

"That's why I gave you that document. Those shares are yours, that company is yours. I respect that. I honor that." He enfolded her within his arms, hugging her lightly.

She kissed him lightly, then said, "But I really want you to be a part of it. That's why I tore up that document you gave me."

He knew he looked stunned. He had been certain nothing meant more to her than her company. His hope had been to come to mean as much to her, in time. "Is that your way of telling me that you love me?"

She looked up at him quickly and he cursed himself for sounding so insecure. But then she smiled, the most beautiful smile he'd ever seen.

"No, that's my way of saying I'd like us to work together. Maybe even, you know, merge. But I do love you, Beau Brannigan, and that's a miracle I never thought to have."

"So maybe, since you love me and all, you wouldn't mind merging more than our companies."

"Maybe."

He flipped her onto her back. One finger stroked the collar—his collar—that she'd worn, just for him. He kissed her, taking her deep, drinking in her unique flavor.

"Brannigan MacLean International has a nice ring to it." He knew his smile was smug.

"I like MacLean Brannigan, myself."

"We'll negotiate."

BEAU AND THE LADY BEAST

THE END

SIREN PUBLISHING

MORGAN ASHBURY

Lily in Bloom

Lily in Bloom

MORGAN ASHBURY
Copyright © 2008

Prologue

He dropped his clothes right in front of her.

Lily should have said something the instant he came into view, but she didn't. Instead, she stepped back just enough to hide in the shadows. And she stood, a silent witness, a hidden voyeur, as he stripped.

The son of her uncle's neighbor, he'd been introduced to her a few days before. Ryan Kincaid was only sixteen.

The moon, bright in a cloudless sky, painted his flesh with silver streaks of light, an incandescent glow that glistened and aroused. His chest, broad and manly, nearly barren of hair, made her mouth water. *He must work hard.* Even from this distance, she could see highly defined muscles. His hands went to the front of his shorts, and a part of Lily's brain told her to look away. As a married thirty-year-old mother of two, she had no right playing voyeur. But held captive by the moonlight, the night, and the glorious sight of this emerging Adonis, she looked on.

The moonlight focused on his completely naked, magnificent form, like a spotlight would a performer on the stage.

Lily forgot the sleeplessness that had chased her from her bed. Seeking only the open air and a chance to dip her feet in the pool on this steamy August night, she'd instead been given a visual erotic temptation.

Lily's nipples beaded beneath her simple cotton nightshirt. Ryan stretched, slowly turning right and then left, performing warm-up exercises that warmed Lily inside and out. Clenching her legs together, she tried to stem the flow of moisture dampening her panties.

She'd been married more than a decade and had never been this aroused. Ryan stretched his hands overhead, bending backwards slightly. Lily's eyes zeroed in on his cock. Fully erect, proud, it called to her, a forbidden call of lust and need. She couldn't help but compare it to Reg's, her husband. How could a sixteen-year-old young man have a larger, more beautiful penis than a fully-grown man? But he did, and she found herself wondering, for the first time in her life, how a cock would taste. Her entire body shivered as she could almost imagine herself on her knees before him, ready to worship that stiff rod with lips and tongue, eager to taste, then to lie back, spread her legs, and...

The sound of a splash pulled her from her sensuous haze. Ryan had dived into the pool, leaving Lily alone and bereft, and more than a little embarrassed. Feeling her face heat in shame, certain the entire world would see her shocking behavior, she slowly crept backwards until, safely around the corner of the house, she could escape. Silently on bare feet, she stole back to her room, closing the door softly behind her. Flinging herself on her bed, she closed her eyes, as if she'd been asleep all along. As if what she had just witnessed had been only a dream, after all.

But it had been real, and the arousal that so recently flooded her didn't abate. Instead, it cried out for release. With hands that trembled, Lily pulled her nightshirt to her waist, and then higher. Her nipples, hard buds, throbbed, and Lily's hands moved over them, caressing, pinching harder. Until that moment, she had no idea her breasts connected to her womb. Her hips surged and her sex burned with hunger. Shocked at her own actions, but unable to stop, her hands wandered down, then under the waistband of her panties.

The first touch of her fingers on her pussy had her clit stiffening and seeking more. Whimpering, Lily pictured Ryan, naked, preening. Imagined him, ready, rising over her. Masturbating for the first time in her life, she gave herself the most delicious orgasm she'd ever experienced.

As she willed sleep to take her, Lily promised herself that, come the dawn, this night's embarrassing activities would only have been a misadventure, now over. She promised herself in the light of a new day, the yearning and lust she'd felt for that young man would be dead and gone.

But it didn't die. It merely lay dormant.

Waiting.

Chapter 1

13 years later

"Hello, Lily."

The black helmet with tinted glass concealed the rider's identity as well as the tight leather of his jacket outlined his chest. If he'd been wearing a cape, she might have imagined him a villain in a space movie. But where the helmet betrayed nothing, the stretched fabric across his chest shouted *MAN*.

Her heart raced. Having a motorcycle roar down her country lane had stirred a primal fear within her. Despite having lived nearly a month in the country, she remained a city girl at heart, with a city girl's fear of bikers and gangs. She'd very nearly bolted for the safety of the house, and locked doors. But the fight or flight dilemma within her had taken a few moments too long to sort out. Now she faced a stranger who seemed to know her name, while his identity remained a mystery.

He took his time, she thought, turning off the bike, removing his gloves. She couldn't take her eyes off him as he slowly reached up and unsnapped the strap that held the protective headgear in place. Almost like slow motion, he lifted the heavy helmet up and off, eyes closed, and shook his head, his long hair dancing on the breeze.

Beautiful.

She'd seen him just a couple of months ago, at Uncle Mark's funeral. He'd been one of the pallbearers. Since her uncle had made all the arrangements, she'd no idea of his name. But even then, he'd seemed familiar to her, somehow.

"Figured it out yet?"

Oh, hell. Memories of a long ago summer washed through her. How could she be aroused and embarrassed at the same time? She felt her cheeks turn red, and wished the Earth would simply open up and swallow her.

"Ryan. I didn't recognize you."

"With my clothes on?"

"Pardon?"

"I meant my riding clothes, of course."

A lively twinkle in his eyes told her he'd been aware of her that night, all those years ago.

Rather than disappear, as she'd prayed the memory would, it had converted itself to a dream that replayed in her sleep, over the years, on the capricious whims of chance.

The last time that dream visited had been just two nights ago.

Nothing to do now but brazen it out. "Of course, you did. How are you?"

"Me? I've been very good. You?"

Oh, she'd never played this game of flirt in her entire life! What possessed her to do so now? He might be a fully-grown man, but more than a decade separated them. They had names for women like her who toyed with young studs.

And no, she told the tiny voice inside her head, *that name is not 'Lucky'.*

"I'm fine, Ryan. Thank you."

He flashed a grin of pure mischief, then swung his right leg over the bike. He set the stand, placed the helmet on the seat, and slowly pulled the zipper down on his leather jacket. Soon that, too, draped the bike, and he stood in front of her, arms akimbo.

Lily tried not to notice the way the thin cotton t-shirt plastered itself against that impressively muscular chest. She told herself she would not look below his waist, and then found herself admiring how the worn denim showcased his powerful thighs.

"Are you going to do the neighborly thing and invite me in...for a drink?"

Her head snapped up, her eyes wide. His grin spread, and she watched him do a slow perusal of her, head to toe. For one long moment, her mind simply refused to work. Then his words penetrated. "Are we neighbors, then?"

He nodded toward the north, and Lily knew he indicated the next farm in that direction.

"Yeah. I've been living on the homestead since before my dad died."

"Oh. I'm sorry. I didn't know he'd died."

"It's been a few years, but thanks. I also spent a lot of time with Mark. As a matter of fact, I made him a promise before he passed."

"Oh?"

"Mmm. I promised him that if you accepted your inheritance and moved in here, I'd keep an eye on you," he took one step forward, then another, his grin nearly feral, "give you a hand, or whatever else you might need. Help you…make it."

Ryan's greater height forced Lily to look up as he came closer. His gaze, intent on her face, flicking down to take in the thrust of her breasts against her tee shirt, heated her blood. His words caressed the inner part of her that had been stirred to awakening the moment she realized his identity. She bit back a groan as her nipples hardened and her sex moistened. Muscles flexed, as if preparing to receive his penis deep into her body.

How could this happen to her? She was no sex kitten! In fact, the last time she'd made love with Reg had been…too long ago to remember.

Grabbing hold of her runaway thoughts, she swallowed, lifted her chin and squared her shoulders. Time for her to stop this ridiculous train of thought, to stop taking everything this young man said in a provocative way, and to come back to the sober, hardworking, and boring woman she knew herself to be.

"You're referring to the farm, of course. That's very kind of you."

"Kindness has nothing to do with it. Actually, I was referring to pleasuring every inch of *you*. But I can help you with the farm, too."

Lily knew she likely resembled a fish feeding on plankton, but she couldn't help it. As Ryan's words echoed in her mind, she could only gape and stare while seized by the almost giddy urge to laugh. She could probably count on the fingers of both hands the number of times her husband had made love to her—*if* she could remember back that far—and this young stud—

"Breathe, Lily."

"You...I...you can't go around saying things like that! Even if you *are* joking, my God, Ryan! That's—"

"I wasn't joking, babe."

Lily found she could do nothing more than just stare at him. With an almost subtle shake of his head, he reached out and grabbed hold, yanking her forward. He didn't just kiss her. He plundered.

One moment, she was living in the real world as she knew it, the next, Lily was lost. Her brain stopped working as Ryan's mouth fastened on hers, as his tongue invaded her mouth and he tickled her tonsils. His scent surrounded her as he held her tight against his solid male body. Enveloped by his arms, she felt drenched in desire. Unable to resist, she opened her mouth wide, her tongue returning his caresses, dancing with his, then racing. Seduced by the taste of morning coffee and man, she gripped his shoulders and held on, because her legs lost all strength. Her nipples hardened into tiny pebbles that burned with the need to be rubbed back and forth against his chest just to survive. The pit of her belly shivered, her uterus contracted all the way to the lips of her pussy, and she felt moisture soak her panties.

She had never been kissed like this in her entire life.

Ryan kept one hand on the back of her head as the other cupped her bottom. He lifted her, it seemed so easy and natural, and grunted when her legs wrapped themselves around him.

"Rub yourself against my cock, honey. Go ahead, take what you need."

"Ryan—" Lily shuddered in his arms at the naked command, and began shaking her head in denial even as her hips rolled forward, stroking her cotton-covered sex against his denim-covered erection.

"Yeah, that's it. Do it again, Lily."

"No, I—" Her saner angels uttered the words automatically, meant to call up sobriety and decorum. But she wrapped her arms more tightly around him, fused her mouth to his, and ground her pelvis against him one more time, and then again and again.

Lily cried out as everything inside her caught fire and erupted in an explosion of sizzling, roaring pleasure. Wave after wave of rapture washed over and through her, sending spasms outward from her pussy until her entire body trembled, out of control. She gasped and gulped and moaned, helpless to do anything else but rub her mound against him. Her brain frantically tried to make sense of what her body felt, but this went far and beyond anything she'd ever experienced. She rested her head on Ryan's shoulder, and as the last of the orgasm faded, a sob wrenched its way out from deep down inside her. Depleted of energy, soaked in shock, she surrendered to it, as well.

* * * *

Ryan continued to kiss and hold her as the ripples of her orgasm raged through her. The taste of her intoxicated him more than he could have imagined. Instantly drunk on her, he wanted only to stay that way. He felt her whimpers and swallowed them, even as his kiss continued to devour her. His cock was extra hard, and he knew he could have fucked her right then and there. He wanted that nearly more than he'd ever wanted anything. Lily Martin had been a fire in his blood since the summer he turned sixteen. But the look of shock on her face when he'd teased her spoke volumes of Lily's inexperience. Her kiss had been awkward and clumsy until she'd surrendered to his possession. Even now, as he held her against his erection, shivering as she came, he realized the woman in his arms had limited sexual experience.

Closing his eyes tightly, he reined in his own desire, stamping down the urge to strip them both naked and plow into her. That moment would come, soon and often if he had anything to say about it. But right now, he needed to focus on Lily. When her cries of pleasure turned to cries of another sort, he continued to hold her, wordless murmurs of comfort rumbling from his throat. Carrying her easily into the house, he settled himself into one of the kitchen chairs, and when Lily tried to get away from him, he switched his hold of her so that he cradled her on his lap like a child.

"Stay, Lily. Just let me hold you."

"Oh, God. I can't believe I just...that I...and you..."

"Shhh. It's all right, babe. Everything's fine. I know you're embarrassed, but you don't have to be. Please stop struggling and let me hold you. Just for another few moments. Then if you want me to let you go, I will."

"I'm ashamed of myself."

"Why? Because you came?"

"I'm a forty-three year old divorced mother of two grown children and I just plastered myself against a man I barely know and behaved like the most wanton nymphomaniac."

"Yeah, and I loved every moment of it. It felt good, didn't it? I made that first move, honey. Hoping for exactly what just happened. Your response to me was so much more wonderful than I ever imagined, and I imagined plenty thinking about you all these years. What happened between us really isn't that much different than masturbating, is it?"

When Lily didn't answer and she hid her head deeper into his chest, Ryan's hands stilled their stroking.

"Lily?"

"I don't. That is, I did, one time. Well—"

"After my strip tease by the pool?"

"Oh."

Ryan had never heard a single two-letter word drawn out in such a mournful tone. It took every bit of his will not to roar in laughter.

"Why had you never masturbated before—or after?"

"Ryan!"

"There's only the two of us here, sweetheart. Just you and me. I've been hot for you since the first time I laid eyes on you. I'm not embarrassed to tell you that I fantasized about you whenever I jerked off—that summer and long after. In the pool that night, I wished with everything in me that you would come out of hiding, strip yourself bare, and get into the water with me. Of course, I knew that wouldn't happen at the time. I was still a kid, and you a married woman. But I'm no longer a kid, and you're no longer married. There's nothing wrong with what we just shared, Lily, unless I make your skin crawl."

Lily's head came up at that and she looked him square in the eyes. "You do not make my skin crawl."

He continued to look at her, one eyebrow raised.

"You want more? I'm sure you know you're gorgeous and sexy as sin. You can't possibly need me to tell you that."

"What I need you to tell me is whether or not you're attracted to me. Whether or not you enjoyed my kissing you. Whether or not you're going to let me lay you down, spread your legs, and fuck you until we're both too weak to walk."

Chapter 2

"You say the most outrageous things."

"It's a gift."

Ryan smiled as Lily erupted in laughter. He smoothed her hair back, shoulder length auburn strands that already hid a few traitorous wisps of gray. Her smooth skin bore no scars or marks of any kind. She'd declared her age as if she was one step from the nursing home, but a man looking at her just now, staring into her greenish hazel eyes, would be hard pressed to peg her at even forty.

To him, she hadn't changed in the thirteen years they'd been apart. He still remembered the first time he'd set eyes on her. He'd immediately classified her as a MILF—mother I'd like to fuck—and had fantasies about her from day one. Now holding her on his lap, he knew reality outshone everything he'd imagined.

"Maybe the words I've spoken seem outrageous to you because no one's ever said them before. And that, Lily, is a damn shame. Your ex-husband must be a real asshole."

"Reg considers himself a man of the world, a connoisseur of fine wines and fine women. In that order. He told me so himself, when he asked for the divorce. The children had grown, and he had done me the tremendous honor, at great personal sacrifice, of allowing me to remain his wife all those years. But he'd found a beautiful young woman more deserving of the title of Mrs. Reginald Martin. And I, being such an asexual creature, couldn't possibly have any objections at this point in my life to dissolving the marriage, and vacating the house."

Ryan knew shocked horror showed on his face.

Lily nodded. "Reginald's version of, 'I want to fuck you.' And I can't believe I just *said* that word."

"He *is* an asshole."

Ryan had listened to Mark go on and on about Reginald Martin. But he'd thought the older man's protests more along the vein of a surrogate father who thought no one quite good enough for his precious daughter.

Ryan had traveled the world, taking five years right after university to indulge his wanderlust. He'd met and enjoyed a lot of women. He'd honed his lover's skills to a fine art. He'd never had a single complaint from any of his partners. And now he knew that all those years he'd been preparing himself for this one woman.

A fanciful notion, that, and one he'd examine in detail later. Right now, he wanted to focus on the woman on his lap. He caressed her arms and waited to see if she would answer the question he'd asked. She looked so troubled he wanted to make everything right for her. *Talk about fanciful notions.*

"I'm not blameless, Ryan. I knew he cheated on me—hell, probably from not long after our honeymoon, and I didn't do anything about it. A bit naïve when we married, I'd been raised with the image of man as head of the house—something that today's young women don't have, and likely can't even fathom. But I never did anything to make things different. I just let it continue on."

"That's a lot of guilt, honey, and I bet you don't really deserve a half of it. I think you *were* young when you got married and good old Reggie did a primo job of demoralizing and conditioning you. I hope you scalped him in the divorce."

"Why do so many people say that? My hairstylist, my lawyer, Uncle Mark…money doesn't make the wrongs go away. It doesn't fix anything. I got the cash settlement that I demanded. I didn't ask for anything more, although I would have liked a few of the furnishings out of the house."

"No, I can see that money isn't important to you. I guess the point would be if money mattered to your ex, then depriving him of great gooey gobs of it might just inflict a measure of pain. In return for all that arrogant bullshit he flung at you all those years."

When she again ducked her head, he used a single finger to lift her face, so he could look into her eyes.

"What?"

"I'm not completely certain that it *was* all bullshit. I only ever did one thing in my life—get married and have kids."

Ryan read her expression and her tone perfectly. "And you think that because you're divorced, you've failed?"

He could see the truth of his words on her face.

"Your husband cheated on you, Lily. He's the one who failed."

"That's not the vibes that Reg has been sending since he announced his intentions. That's certainly not what my mother thinks. And that's not how it feels."

And there, Ryan knew, lay the crux of the matter. Lily *felt* like a loser. She had absolutely no self-confidence as a person, or as a woman.

His feelings for her had never been just physical. He'd watched her that summer all those years ago—watched how she treated her uncle, and her unappreciative kids. She had a kindness and compassion within her that had drawn him when he'd been a sixteen-year-old boy still missing the touch of a loving mother, by then dead five years. And from what Mark had said from time to time in the years since, Lily continued to give of herself to people who treated her gift of service as less than nothing.

He wanted her body, yes. But he wanted her heart and soul as well. He had his work cut out for him. A smile ghosted across his face. *Definitely worth the effort.*

"You never did answer my questions."

Lily cocked her head to one side, puzzlement on her face.

"Are you attracted to me? Did you enjoy kissing me? Are you going to let me have you?"

* * * *

Lily suddenly realized that she still sat on Ryan's lap. The incredible heat of him seeped through her clothes and into her flesh. Her ass felt hot, and she resisted the urge to twitch it. Pressing against the edge of her hip, his erection grew harder. She'd had an orgasm, but he hadn't. Funny how that little fact had slipped her mind until now.

Ever since that one night thirteen years ago, Ryan had been in her thoughts. Oh, not a constant presence, to be sure. But the dream would come, haunt her, and she'd think of him. In her dream, of course, he remained untouchable. He'd been a teen, little more than a child, and her craving for him shamed her, then and now, when she remembered it. A child no longer, she found herself very much liking the man he had grown into.

It seemed strange to Lily that she had no difficulty talking to Ryan, a man she barely knew, about the most personal of topics. She felt a sort of connection to him, a comfort with him that, all things considered, was remarkable.

She saw he waited for an answer, so she said the first thing on her mind. "I never thought I would ever have sex again."

The look he gave her communicated patience. He deserved an explanation, not only for her answer but her actions. How could she explain to him what she'd been thinking these last few months since the divorce? Still, unbelievable as it may seem, she felt closer to Ryan Kincaid than she'd ever felt to anyone.

Lily had never excelled at making friendships with other women. Discouraged from holding a job or pursuing a career not only by her old-fashioned mother but also by a husband who wanted his wife's attention focused solely on himself and his home, Lily had never built that independent identity most modern women enjoyed and took for granted. Moving from her mother's house to her husband's, not even bothering to go to university, adult female relationships had been rare for her. Mostly, she just kept to herself.

Her relationship with her kids hadn't fared much better. Somehow, she'd never quite managed to be in control there, either. Oh, she cared for them and had performed all the countless tasks she knew mothers did. She loved her children, almost too much at times, she thought recently. When she and Reg divorced, her grown son and daughter had opted to stay with the parent paying their university tuitions. She didn't resent their choice—though she did wish they had been less effusive in their acceptance of their father's new wife.

So here she sat, forty-three and essentially alone in life. Did that make her even more susceptible to Ryan's charms?

She'd been silent too long. When she met Ryan's eyes, she saw a tenderness there that brought a lump to her throat. Then he caressed her cheek, and his look turned lascivious.

"Why don't we start where we left off, all those years ago?" he asked, his voice husky with intent. "Let's go back to that fantasy and play it out. I want you naked and wet—inside and out."

She gasped when he grabbed the bottom of her shirt and pulled it over her head. She had to work at keeping her hands from covering her breasts when Ryan removed her bra. What had happened between them, to this point, could be considered a simple lapse of control, a single episode of heavy petting. No real lines had been crossed. But if things continued on this way, more than heavy petting was on the agenda. If things continued on, she would have sex with Ryan Kincaid. Very, very soon.

The possibility of having an affair, of taking a lover, had really never before occurred to her. She'd fully believed herself an asexual woman. But now the possibility of an affair seemed a certainty, and the knowledge that an entire world of sensuality awaited her discovery...

Lily moistened dry lips. She could think of no reason to deny herself the pleasure awaiting her.

"I've never gone swimming naked."

Ryan caressed her breasts, his smile slow and devastating.

"I have a feeling there's a lot you've never done, Lily." He gathered her close and kissed her, long and deep. "There's an awful lot I can share with you...show you. If you want me to."

Lily didn't want to think. She just wanted to kiss him again. Leaning forward, wrapping her arms around him, she fused her mouth to his.

She'd never initiated a kiss before, so she didn't know what she expected. Ryan's open-mouthed surrender delighted her. Indulging herself fully, she used her tongue to explore his taste completely. A low fire burning in the pit of her belly told her one orgasm hadn't been enough. Giving in to the urge she'd experienced earlier, she brushed her breasts back and forth across his chest. Her nipples hardened painfully, and she felt more than heard her whimper. A basic unspoken female plea for more, it galvanized Ryan into growling into her mouth. His fingers sought and found the pebbled points of her breasts and rolled them between his forefingers and thumbs, squeezing lightly.

Lily wanted, more than anything, to take this gorgeous man up on his offer. Yes, those fourteen years still stretched between them. But Ryan, a man fully grown, like she, was unattached. It wasn't as if they were considering having a serious relationship. But an affair? Why not?

"Do I take that as a yes?" Ryan asked when she relinquished his mouth.

She slowly pulled back, smiling, her arms still looped around his neck.

"Ryan?"

"Yes, Lily?"

"I want you to show me *everything*."

Chapter 3

Only two men had ever seen Lily naked—Reg, and her doctor. Not once in her life had she ever been naked in the great outdoors. If she ever imagined such a thing, she would have imagined it happening in the dead dark of night, with only the stars—maybe—as witnesses.

That she would be naked in full view of a man she barely knew just shy of noon on a bright and sunny Wednesday didn't seem real. Self-consciousness about her body flooded her. She'd carried and borne two children. Her belly hadn't been flat or her abs tight in years. Her breasts, though neither tiny nor fulsome, could no longer be called pert. Yet Ryan seemed to like the view. Then the next instant, her thoughts scattered as he shed the last of his clothes.

Ryan, naked at sixteen, had been an eyeful. As an adult, he was much, much more. Magnificent, with a tanned, muscled chest, broad shoulders and lean hips, he appeared so much more *man* than she'd ever seen. His chest, lightly dusted with hair the same rich chestnut brown as the mane that nearly brushed his shoulders, tempted her fingers to explore. His legs, corded and strong, stood braced, defiant. Her eyes riveted on his penis, and she felt herself get wet in response to the sheer beauty of it. She'd rarely looked at Reg's cock, finding the sight of it, aroused or flaccid, to be repugnant. Her response to this shaft puzzled her. Ryan's was longer and thicker than her ex's. Fully aroused, the organ stretched upward just past his navel, proud and hard and delicious.

Her gaze shot up to his face when she realized she'd been staring at him for a long, silent time. Saying nothing, Ryan smiled and held out his hand.

Nervous, yet compelled, Lily put her hand in his and followed as he led her outside and to the pool.

The water looked clear and clean, the temperature just warm enough to be refreshing without being cold. She watched as Ryan dove neatly into the deep end. He surfaced, shook his wet hair back, and smiled.

"Come on, gorgeous. Get that sweet ass of yours in here."

Lily didn't think about it, she just dove in, surfacing close to him. He didn't make a grab for her, which is what she thought might happen next. Instead, he began to swim laps, taking her by surprise. Treading water, she watched him pass her twice before deciding to join him.

The feeling of absolute freedom astonished her. She nearly giggled at the sensation of her boobs, buoyant and surrounded by water. Feeling light and sexy and free, her movements as she slipped into a front crawl became smoother and faster than if she'd been wearing her suit. Soon, she forgot her nudity, forgot she wasn't alone. The exercise worked its magic. Her body began to release tension she didn't even know she carried. The silkiness of the water caressing her flesh relaxed her body, energized her mind. When she tired, she slipped onto her back and simply floated. *This is what freedom is really all about. Why have I never done this before?*

"Everything, huh?"

The single word hung on the air, so casually asked anyone else would have just made a sound in either agreement or dissent. How could she already know him so well as to understand this was an important moment? Drawing her feet downward, Lily treaded water. He stood waist deep, leaning against the side of the pool, watching her.

"I didn't know I could feel the way I felt earlier, when you kissed me. So, yes, I want to find out what else I've been missing."

"'Everything' is a pretty big word, babe. There's mainstream fucking. And then there's…a whole lot more."

"More?" The word emerged as an excited whisper, and Lily had to lick her lips to relieve the sudden dryness there. When Ryan's eyes flared at the action, her senses went on full alert.

"Yeah." He left the side of the pool and approached her, she imagined the way a jungle cat stalks unsuspecting prey.

Unable to stop herself, she backed up in the water until the solid concrete of the edge nudged against her back. His gaze never leaving hers, he followed, stopping when mere inches separated them.

There was nothing gentle in the way Ryan grabbed her hair, pulled her head back so that he could meld his lips to hers. No wooing in the way his tongue stabbed into her mouth and dominated hers. Nothing subtle in the plunging of his fingers into her pussy, two fingers that felt like two hundred in the resulting stretch and sting. And yet, despite the roughness of his possession, her body responded with heart-racing, breath-heaving arousal. The sting eased almost instantly as moisture coated the fingers within. Ryan began to piston them in and out faster and deeper.

"You're so tight, baby."

"More," she panted, breaking the kiss and instinctively raising her hips and spreading her legs to give him easier access. She thought she might go mad if he didn't keep finger-fucking her.

Instead of complying, his hand went still and he placed a light kiss on her lips.

"You'll get more. You'll get everything, if that's really what you want."

"Please...I need..."

"I know what you need, Lily. And you'll get it, very soon. Come on, let's go inside."

* * * *

He smiled when Lily's blissful sigh echoed against the walls of the shower as his soapy hands caressed her breasts. Leaning against him, back to chest, he felt her give herself over to his ministrations. A shiver wracked her when his tongue sampled her ear. His warm chuckle caused another.

"Everything?"

"You keep saying that."

"Well, it's kind of right out there, you know?"

"I guess it is."

"So tell me...have you ever had a lover's tongue here?"

Lily gasped when his fingers stroked her slit, teasing her clitoris.

"No."

"Have you ever been tied to the bed by a lover?"

"No."

"Have you ever taken a lover's cock into your mouth? Or received it...here?"

She moaned in pure desire when he rubbed his hard shaft against her bottom.

"N...no."

"Oh, Lily, all your firsts are going to be with me, babe."

It took only moments to rinse, and then he dried them both quickly. Lily wrapped her arms around Ryan's neck when he picked her up and carried her to her bed. He'd taken a moment before they got into the shower to place the condoms he'd brought with him on her bedside table. Grabbing one, he tore the package open, prepared himself quickly. Then she pulled him toward her as she spread her legs wide and lifted her hips.

Ryan carefully placed the tip of his cock on her opening and began to push. The extended foreplay had kept her wet. He'd done what he could to stretch her with his fingers, but Lily had the tightest pussy he'd ever taken, and he was a big boy.

A tiny mew of feminine distress froze him in his place. "You can take me, sweetheart. I'll be as gentle as I can." He gritted his teeth and pressed forward, the warm wet welcome already so fabulous he just wanted to thrust hard and deep, and keep on doing so. It took every bit of will he could summon to deny himself that instant pleasure.

Instead, taking her mouth in a searing kiss, he stoked her breasts. He held his penis steady, just the head of it within her, and took the time to get her hotter and wetter. She raised her hips and he reached down and stroked her clit. Taking her needy sounds as his cue, he resumed his penetration. This time, he buried himself to the hilt.

"So...good." Lily sighed, wrapping her arms and legs around him.

"Hang on, baby. I need to..."

"Yes!"

He took her as he'd longed to take her, the hard steady thrusts of his cock powerful enough to shake the bed. She responded gloriously, clinging even as she worked her hips in sync with his, hot and giving, as he'd somehow known she would be. He held on to his will, wanting more than anything to just keep thrusting in her, thrusting and thrusting without cessation. His cock began to twitch, and he knew his climax neared.

"Kiss me, Lily. I want my tongue in your mouth when I come."

* * * *

Everything about sex with Ryan was so much more than she could have imagined. His words in the shower, designed to arouse and maybe frighten just a little, had lit her fires, and clenched her gut. The weight of him pressing her into the bed excited her. He'd taken her in a complete, all-out, hell-bent-for-leather mating that she thought—and hoped—would leave marks. Hot full friction, Lily had never felt anything so good in all her life. Everything disappeared then, except Ryan and the salacious sensations racing through her. She thrust her hips counter point to his, a racing pace now, and felt the orgasm gathering at the base of her uterus. Crying out in pure rapture, she held on tight as the tidal wave flooded her body and drenched her soul. She vaguely heard Ryan swear, as he held her bottom close, pressing their bodies more tightly together. Aware of his hot penis pulsing within her, contentment filled her to overflowing.

For long minutes, only the sound of gasping breathing could be heard. Lily felt Ryan's weight on her and considered him the best blanket she'd ever worn.

"You okay, sweetheart?" His question, a husky whisper, tickled her ear.

"You tell me."

"You're fucking fabulous. I didn't hurt you? I thought I got a bit rough. I might have bruised you."

She groaned as he moved off her, and then smiled when he simply rolled to his side and held her close.

"I certainly hope so. That way, if I begin to doubt this actually happened—you know, if I wake up afraid I just had another dream—a mark or two would be wonderful reassurance."

"You are an amazing woman. Wanna snuggle for a while?"

"Aren't we?"

"Mmm. Just wanted to make sure you didn't have anything else you needed to do."

"The only thing that comes to mind is a repeat performance."

"Nap. Then food. Then we'll see what we can do about that."

"Sounds good."

* * * *

"I could make some sandwiches," she offered as they descended the stairs an hour later.

"That would be great. Let's eat outside. After lunch, we can relax in the hammock. Once I put it up, that is."

"You have a hammock?"

Ryan chuckled. "No, babe, you do. It's in the shed. Mark bought it last year, and told me later that he regretted not getting one sooner."

Ryan tied off the last rope as Lily came out the back door, balancing a tray. He quickly relieved her of the weight of it, carrying it to the picnic table while she took a moment to look at his handiwork.

"It looks complicated. How the heck do you get into it?"

"You sort of just fall into it. And they're a bit hard to get out of. Which is, I believe, the way it should be."

Lily had donned her bathing suit. Ryan didn't tease her for being too shy to sit around, eating while naked. In fact, he'd kissed her lightly, and slipped on his boxers. When they got into the pool again, he figured he could talk her out of her suit without a problem.

"So what is it that you do, exactly?" Lily poured some iced tea into her glass, then offered the pitcher to Ryan.

"As little as possible."

When she continued to just look at him, Ryan smiled. "You'd be amazed how often that line is enough. Actually, I work out of my house. Software." He wasn't going to go into the details of it. In his experience, most people's eyes glazed over when it came to the technical-speak of software design. He didn't feel the need to puff himself up in her eyes, either. He had more money than he would ever spend, and seemed to be able to keep selling his designs so would continue to have more money than he would ever spend. Lily had already given him her opinion of money, so he didn't bother.

"I don't do anything."

"Is this a problem?"

"Well, I should, don't you think? I'm forty-three years old, and I've never held a job. In all likelihood, I have several decades left to live. I should do something to pass the time, shouldn't I?"

"I don't know." He chewed the ham and cheese sandwich slowly, pondering her question.

"Do you need to earn an income to keep a roof over your head and body and soul together?"

"Not really. The farm is mine, free and clear. The only expenses I have are utilities and taxes. I have no debts. I invested my divorce settlement, and the money Uncle Mark left me, so I have a good monthly income. I'd also managed to have a nice savings account of my own accumulated before the divorce."

Ryan cocked one eyebrow, because she said that with a smirk, which intrigued him.

"Shortly after we got married, Reg made sure to give me 'pin money' every week. An allowance, if you will."

"An...allowance. As if you were what...his kid? His...servant?"

"Reg is many things, but a twenty-first century man is not one of them. Anyway, I began socking that away when I found out about the first mistress, rather than using it for whatever he imagined I spent it on. Of course, being a fair man—his perception, not mine—he made sure that I got a small 'raise' each year. I still had a bank account in my maiden name, so I put my savings there. Neither of the lawyers bothered to ask if I had any independent assets, nor conducted any kind of a search to see if I did. So, golly, it just never came up during the divorce proceedings."

"I'm guessing it's substantial. You got a bit of your own back after all, didn't you?"

"A bit."

"So, you don't have to work. Why, then, would you want to?"

"Personal growth?"

"You really feel 'less than' in that way, don't you?"

"Yeah. I know it sounds foolish."

"No, it doesn't sound foolish. I think it would be damn near impossible to have a really positive image of yourself if you've been put down most of your life."

"You and Uncle Mark really did talk a lot, huh? He always thought I had been treated so much worse than I thought I was. I got to live in a nice home, drive a nice car, do pretty much what I wanted to do as long as I took care of the house, and Reg."

Ryan could have pressed the issue. And probably, knowing himself as well as he did, he would. Once Lily became more comfortable with him. But for now, he wanted to erase the worried look from her face. Two ways that he knew to do that. One, fuck her brains out. Two, reassure her. First the second, then the first.

"Well, you don't need to have a job to achieve personal growth. But you do need to have a plan."

Chapter 4

Lily didn't understand how forming a plan for personal growth necessitated a trip into the city to go shopping, but then she could admit she didn't understand a lot of things. Saturday morning, bright and early, Ryan arrived. He parked his bike in the barn, then came into the house to 'help Lily get dressed.' His version of help involved stripping them both naked, having his way with her, and then showering them both and starting the dressing process again at the beginning.

"I have to wear panties," Lily protested, even as Ryan stood in front of the drawer, blocking her access to it.

"No, you don't."

"I can't wear a skirt into the city with no underwear underneath of it."

"Sure you can. The same way that you can wear this nice t-shirt with no bra."

"Ryan!"

"Come on, Lily. It'll be fun."

When she only continued to stare at him, he gave her his best smile and what he must have considered the no-fail argument. "No one else will ever know. Besides, it'll really turn me on. Unless, of course, you're too chicken."

She slipped on her red and white cotton skirt, and the red cotton t-shirt. Studying herself in the mirror, she had to admit that it wasn't obvious, this lack of underwear. The shirt fit loosely enough and her breasts were small enough that it wasn't overtly obvious she went braless.

"I feel so…"

"Naked?"

"Yeah."

"That's the point, sweetheart." He pulled her into his arms and kissed her lavishly. "Every time you remember that you're naked under your skirt, remember that when we get home, I'm going to put my mouth on your pussy and drive you wild."

She didn't have to check the mirror to see if she wore a blush, beet red, to match her outfit. She could feel that she did.

* * * *

"I should probably tell you right up front. I've never really liked shopping."

Ryan had accepted the keys to Lily's car and was behind the wheel, navigating their way toward the city. At her confession, he shot her a quick look to judge her mood. He'd thought she'd been joking. But her expression belied that.

"Why not, babe?"

"What's to like? You stop what you're doing, drive to the mall, deal with the crowds, try to guess what to buy, drag it home, discover it's just not *quite* right, then have to go back and repeat the process, but add in the always fun getting-a-refund, first. Waste of time, if you ask me."

There had been more than a trace of heat in Lily's words. He had enough knowledge of the lady beside him, and her family, to guess they'd never appreciated her efforts on their behalf. Now, he understood the lack of stuff at her place. He'd snooped shamelessly yesterday when she'd been napping. She had very little in the way of clothing, make-up, or jewelry. She had no computer, no DVD or VCR, no CD player. Some photos decorated the rooms—her kids, her kids and her ex-husband, her uncle, her mother. But no art hung on the walls, and she had no pretty little do-nothings scattered about.

Shopping had been turned into just one more thing to do and get criticized for, he realized.

"If you hate shopping, then why did you agree to go with me today?"

"To please you."

Wow. For the first time, Ryan understood the magnitude of what Lily had lived—and the battle ahead of him. As much as it warmed him deep inside to know she'd do something she hated *just* to please him, it bothered him that she'd acted out of habit—or conditioning. Checking his mirrors, he signaled and pulled the car off the road, onto the shoulder. Once he put it in park, he turned, unclasped her seatbelt, and scooped her into a kiss.

"Thank you. But for the next little while, if you don't mind, we're going to focus on pleasing you for a change. Okay?"

"In just the last few days, you've given me more pleasure than I've ever had before. If I become any more pleased, I'll burst. I don't need anything else."

"Oh, yes, you do. You told me that you wanted to grow, as a person."

"Well, yes…"

"To grow means to experience new stuff, right? To expand your horizons. Right?"

"Right."

He heard the caution in her response and grinned. "Okay, so the first lesson is this: Sometimes it is a fine thing to be selfish."

"Not if you talk to my mother. If you ask her, and my ex, that's always been my biggest flaw."

"Nope. Your biggest flaw is that you don't see yourself clearly, and don't value yourself nearly enough."

* * * *

Ryan's pronouncement had left her speechless

He didn't take her to Hamilton, the closest city. Nor did he settle for Burlington or Oakville. When he left the expressway at the Highway 10 exit in Mississauga, her brow furrowed.

"Square One?"

"Yeah. They've got everything…well, almost everything. There are two more stops we'll have to make after here."

He parked the car in a spot on the second floor of the parking deck attached to one of the larger department stores in the mall, the Bay. As teens, both her children had thought this mall *the* place to shop. She wondered now if that fact had kept her away from here until today.

"This place is huge!"

"Largest mall in the province. Second largest in all of Canada. There's nearly four hundred stores and services here, babe."

"Shop a lot, do you?"

"When I'm in the mood."

"You must be an expert if you know how many stores and services there are here."

Ryan gave her his cheeky grin. "I surfed the web last night, trying to decide where we'd go today. I checked out their website."

"Oh."

Despite his little speech in the car, Lily didn't understand that they had come here to shop for *her*. But she figured it out when he pulled her into a store called La Senza.

"Oh, my." The delicate, lacy bras and nightgowns captivated her. She wanted to go and take a closer look at the pale, frothy creations, far fancier than anything she'd ever owned. She watched in horrified fascination as Ryan's attention zeroed in on some corsets, merry widows, and other bits of kindling in bold, kick-ass colors.

"Oh, but I think pastels look better on me."

"Who told you that?"

She opened her mouth to answer, then snapped it closed again. Over the years, whenever Reg—or her mother for that matter—had bought her a nightgown or lingerie as a gift, it had always been in pastels.

"Uh huh." He read the answer in her eyes. "Tell you what. You buy what you like and I'll buy what I like. Deal?"

"I don't think they carry your size here."

He grinned in appreciation and swooped in for a quick kiss, turning her so she backed tight against a rack of nightgowns, while his hand stroked her hip. Before the kiss ended, his fingers snuck down, then up under her skirt, caressing her naked bottom.

Leaving her with a wink, he headed toward the boudoir apparel that had captured his interest.

Lily stared dumbly at the lingerie before her, trying to get her body back under control. *This is interesting.* She wasn't even wearing panties she could soak. Bearing down, she ordered her libido to take a break, turning her attention fully to the garments. It *had* been a long time since she'd purchased anything for herself. And, she had a new lover. A new, *younger* lover. If that wasn't a cause to splurge on sexy undergarments, she didn't know what was.

"May I help you?"

The clerk appeared to be in her thirties, curvy, and wore a big smile. With a look over her shoulder to where Ryan plowed through the racks unassisted, Lily turned her attention to the young woman, nodded, and surrendered to the urge.

"Yes, as a matter of fact, you can. I think I need...everything."

* * * *

"Five hundred dollars. I just spent *five hundred dollars* on lingerie."

"Amateur."

The scoffing tone stopped Lily in her tracks.

"What do you mean...amateur?"

"You only paid five hundred dollars, babe. We spent an entire half hour in there. A seasoned shopper would have done better than that."

She looked from his Cheshire-cat grin to the bag he held—a bag smaller than her own.

"Tell me you didn't spend more than five hundred just now!"

"No can do."

"Ryan! I can't let you spend that kind of money on me!"

He silenced her with a kiss. "Didn't. I spent it on me. I am going to enjoy dressing you up and then stripping you down. I think it could become my all-time favorite leisure activity."

"What am I going to do with you?"

"Oh, sweetheart, the list is endless."

Lily didn't have time to focus on that outrageous statement. Ryan had a definite agenda in mind as he led her from store to store, one end of the gigantic mall to the other, and from the lower level to the upper one and back down again. They went toe to toe for a few minutes, arguing over who would pay for the purchases. Ryan insisted that since this had been all his idea, he should be the one to foot the bill. Lily argued that while she would accept the lingerie he'd just bought as a gift, no way would she accept anything more. Finally, he gave in, and Lily felt flushed from the victory. Precious few times had she ever stuck to her guns and argued without giving in, let alone won. After seeing the different garments he'd thought suited her, she did give in and told him he could decide what those purchases would be.

He evidently took her confidence in him to heart, and selected several outfits for her, everything from the laid-back casual to the sophisticated chic. He pulled her into the Gap, and Fairweather. They toured and purchased from the Bay and Sears. He took her into Nine West and wasn't happy until she'd chosen *five* pairs of shoes.

"I've never owned five pairs of shoes at one time in my entire life!"

"See, look at all the ground-breaking moments you're having today. And here comes another one."

He led her into the next store, and knew in this one exactly what to buy.

"Why do I need a computer?"

"Everyone needs a computer, Lily. It's the great convenience of the new millennium. You can find out any information, acquire any commodity, pay any bill, play any game, meet people the world over—all from the comfort of your own home."

"But the Internet is just full of—" she almost said sex and spam, but changed her mind. After all, she had taken a younger man as her lover and urged him to show her 'everything.' Complaining about all the sex swirling around on the Internet would be disingenuous.

He seemed to know what she'd been going to say, anyway. "I can't argue that there is a lot on the Internet that you probably won't be interested in, Lily. But the truth is that pretty soon, anyone who doesn't have a computer, or know how to operate one, will be considered functionally illiterate."

"That's a bit harsh, isn't it?"

"No, it's just another sign of the times. A few decades ago, some big wig with IBM declared that there would never be a need for anyone to have a computer in their home. Today it almost seems as if there are more computers in the average home than there are people."

"I must be old. There are days when I feel everything is moving too quickly."

"You're not that old. I feel the same way. Come on, I know just what to get you, and I'll help you learn how to use it."

By the time they left the computer store, Lily imagined her eyes to be permanently crossed. She didn't hold out much hope this old dog could be taught all those new tricks, but she did want to expand her horizons. When even every truck on the highway sported a website reference, obviously computer literacy *was* the new literacy, just as Ryan said.

They detoured to the car to drop off their stuff, then headed to the bar and grill for lunch. As they sipped their drinks, relaxing, the sound ringing close-by interrupted them.

"Is that me, or you?" Ryan asked even as he reached for his cell phone.

"Has to be you. I don't have one."

"You're kidding." He looked up from his phone, pressed a couple of buttons, then slipped it back into his pocket.

"No, I'm not kidding. Aren't you going to answer that?"

"No, it'll take a message and I can get back to him later. How come you don't have a cell phone?"

"Well, the good thing about a cell phone is that you're never out of touch. And the bad thing about a cell phone is that you're never out of touch."

"Ha, ha. You should have one, Lily."

"Oh, I'm not important enough to have one. There's never anyone I need to call that I can't wait until I get home to do so."

"Fine, but you live out in the country, and sometimes you drive into the city. Maybe you have a doctor's appointment and you're stuck in traffic. You can call, tell them you're running late. Besides, you're alone in your car, traveling about. What if your car breaks down and you're stranded? With a cell phone, you can get help. Also, sometimes where we live, the power goes out, and that can mean the phones, too. You should just have one, if only for safety's sake."

Ryan's tone brooked no argument, and Lily bet she could guess their next destination after lunch.

In the end, she decided not to argue the point. She *should* have a cell phone for safety's sake. Ryan had that right. One of the things she always dreaded was being stuck in the middle of nowhere if the car broke down. This way, she could lock her doors and call the auto club if she needed to. So when they walked into a store called Bell World, she had a smile on her face and a positive attitude. She wasn't certain she needed a cell phone that could connect to the Internet, play hundreds of tunes, or take pictures, but in light of the number of horizons she'd already breached today, she let it go.

She left the mall in an amazingly good mood, if much lighter of pocket, prepared for almost anything.

Except, of course, for their next destination.

Chapter 5

"Close your mouth, darling. You look like a fish."

She could hear the chuckle in his voice, and though she wasn't looking at him, she knew he studied her carefully.

"I think I just heard the sound of another horizon being breeched," he said, sounding pleased.

"Ryan, I've never been in one of these places before!"

He leaned over, closer to her. "Why are you whispering?"

"Well…well…*because.*"

"Okay. I'm sensing culture shock, here. Let's begin with the familiar. Let's begin with the clothing."

Very unusual garments, Lily thought moments later. When she'd seen the sign over the door of the tiny shop in the strip mall, she thought more computers, or video games or other gadgets. Ryan seemed to be a man who loved and appreciated such things. Certainly this store sold videos and gadgets, but *Toys for Big Girls and Boys* was all about one game, and one game only: Sex.

"Those panties are missing something," she commented as Ryan held up a tiny hanger he'd taken off the rack.

"Yeah. Great, aren't they?" Ryan grinned and raised his eyebrows in such a way as he held up the crotchless panties that Lilly found herself laughing.

"And they have a matching bra."

"Matching is right. There are holes in these garments, Ryan."

"Like I said, great. What about one of these?" He held up a corset, or what she thought might be a corset, but if she put it on, her breasts would be totally uncovered—and pushed up considerably.

"I don't know…"

"Everything, you said."

"That word is beginning to haunt me."

He showed her the costumes for 'role playing' games. She could be a nurse, a French maid, or, good grief, a schoolgirl! She thought he must have been waiting for her shock to reach a certain level, for then he led her over to some of the accessories. She saw massage oil that purported to taste like strawberries, as well as others that boasted 'tingling' and 'heating' properties. Ryan scooped one of each, letting her know with just a look that they were going to be used very soon.

She didn't need anyone to tell her the purpose of dildos, though she had no idea they would be so life-like, and so large. One was really long, with a head at each end, and her face colored even as she realized it would be used between girlfriends. She frowned when she noticed smaller, cone shaped appliances, pink or purple jelled ones that seemed to be on a stand of some sort. She turned a questioning look to Ryan, then leaned forward and read the package.

"Butt plugs? You mean you put them…"

"Next best thing to having two lovers," he whispered softly.

Lily was speechless.

Her eyes widened when he led her to the back of the shop. As she realized the type of 'toys' in this section, he stood behind her and put his arms around her.

"We won't buy any of these today. But I want you to think about them. I want you to think about whether or not you'd like me to use any of these on you. Or if you'd like to try them out on me. Just think about it for now. I know you need more time to trust me completely."

"I do trust you completely." The words slipped out, unbidden. Lily had heard things over the years. She hadn't lived in a *complete* bubble. The letters BDS&M weren't totally foreign to her, though she didn't know a lot and had certainly never experienced anything like it. As recently as this morning she would have sworn the prospect of being blindfolded or manacled, of having Ryan wield a paddle or a strap on any part of her body—however lightly—would be repugnant. But standing in this store, with Ryan tight against her back, the sensation of his hardened, clothing-restricted cock pressing against her, looking at these items, aroused her.

Ryan must have known how she felt. Bending close, he whispered in her ear even as the fingers of one hand slipped under her shirt to pull and squeeze her hardened nipples.

"You turned on?"

Lily found speech beyond her and simply nodded.

"Because you want to use these on me?"

She shook her head, and had to stifle a groan as Ryan tongued her ear.

"You turned on thinking of me using them on you?"

Again she nodded.

"It wouldn't be just play-acting, love. A little bit of pain goes a hell of a long way towards enhancing pleasure. You will be tied. You will be blindfolded. You will have no control, whatsoever. But it won't be without your consent. I will use something on you—probably a paddle to start. But I promise you this. I'll make it safe for you, give you a way so that if you want me to stop, I will. Still game?"

Oh, Lord, she thought, if he said much more she would come right there and then. How could she want this so badly? Maybe, she thought, bondage only aroused her in the abstract. Maybe once she experienced it, she'd change her mind. And if she did, she knew Ryan would stop. She swallowed heavily, and said, clearly, "Yes."

"All right, then. We'll experiment very soon, sweetheart. Give you a tiny taste, see if you like it. Let's buy these oils and leave. There's one more stop I want to make before we go back to your place."

"Okay." Lily forced her voice to sound stronger.

"And Lily? When we get back to your place, I'm planning to feast on strawberries."

* * * *

Ryan parked on Front Street in downtown Toronto. Shooting Lily a glance, he smiled. She'd been quiet since leaving the sex shop, and he could only hope her thinking centered around the two of them together. As soon as he turned off the car, she roused and looked around.

"Harley-Davidson. Isn't that what your motorcycle is?"

"Yes, ma'am."

He nodded to the man behind the cash register, and with Lily's hand in his, they headed straight over to shelves displaying helmets.

He examined a couple before picking one almost identical to his own.

"You need a new helmet?"

"No."

He turned and handed it to her. "Try it on."

"Me? Why?"

"Ah...to see how it fits?"

"But I don't need a motorcycle helmet."

"Yes, you do, as there are helmet laws in this province. Besides, skin versus pavement, pavement wins, so we're not only getting you a helmet but a full set of leathers, too."

"I'm not going to ride your motorcycle."

"Well, I had thought we would look into getting you one of your own, but later. Come on, Lily—"

Lily held up her hand, cutting him off. "Let me guess. It'll be fun. Right?"

"Right."

"Do you promise to just take me around in the yard the first time? Very slowly. Till I get used to it?"

"Sweetheart...are you scared to ride my Hog?"

"Bet your ass I am. Never been on one of those things in my life. But I'm willing to try if you promise..."

"I promise."

She found the leather pants and jacket he picked out for her to be comfortable, if a little restricting. She knew she'd wear these clothes just for riding, not for lounging in. She found herself admiring the chaps, and thought they would be less difficult to move in. But in the end, she stayed with the one pair of pants and single jacket. The gloves felt a bit awkward, and she couldn't say they facilitated movement, either. But she could see how the outfit would protect her in case of a fall. Ryan had her try on the entire outfit together. She thanked him for snagging a pair of panties out of her La Senza bag before they'd entered the store, and even agreed to his condition—that she hand them back before they returned to the car.

"Who is this space alien?" she asked, as she looked at herself in the store's full-length mirror.

The sales clerk snickered, but continued with Ryan making sure everything fit well.

"My God, what a day," Lily muttered as she headed back to the change room.

* * * *

"Lily, would you do me a favor, please?"

"Mmm?"

"Lift your skirt to your waist, and spread your legs wide. I want to look at you."

Only a few minutes from home, Ryan voiced that stunning request. The late afternoon sun dappled through the trees onto the winding country road. Barely any traffic traveled here this time of day, because most of the local residents commuted to the city to work, or farmed their own land.

"You want me to expose myself to you?"

"Yes, please."

Lily licked dry lips and considered for just a moment. Then slowly, she raised her skirt, lifting her bottom to pull it out from under her, and did exactly what Ryan had asked.

"Sweet," he said, then took his right hand from the steering wheel just for a moment, to stroke her lightly once.

"Sweet and wet."

"You've had me wet all day." Her voice shook with the confession.

"Good. How about we swim first?"

"I'd rather just have you."

She'd never said anything so bold. The words freed her, somehow. Sensing the importance of her declaration, Ryan stroked her once more.

"Oh, you're going to have me. All night long. But I'd really like to get naked and wet with you in the pool, first."

"You want to play with me?"

"There's no one else I'd rather play with."

The next instant, Ryan frowned. Lily followed his line of sight.

"Looks like you have company."

"Oh, my gosh."

Ryan chuckled, watching her scramble to pull her skirt down, only laughing harder when she lightly punched him in the arm.

"It's not funny. That's my son's car. I wonder why he's here?"

"To visit?"

"Well, that would be a first. He hasn't come to see me since I moved out of his father's house, five months ago."

* * * *

Ryan thought about what Lily had just revealed when he brought the car to a stop. They both had their doors opened, but Lily was still seated when her son accosted her.

"Where the hell have you been? I've been waiting here for nearly twenty minutes!"

Lily's face flushed red but not, as Ryan supposed, in indignation at the tone.

"I'm sorry, sweetheart. I had no idea you planned to visit me today. How are you, honey?"

Guilt creased Lily's face as she reached forward to hug her son, and even more when that effort netted her a stiff response.

"Like you care. You haven't come to visit, or even called since you left the city and ran away to here."

Lily reached forward to brush a stray strand of hair off his face. Ryan tried not to let the petulant tone bother him. John Martin acted like a spoiled child, instead of a man of more than twenty.

"You know I can't really come over to the house to see you or your sister, John. That's Mary's house, now. And I have called, but you're never there. You and Alice are always welcome here. Why don't you come inside and I'll make us some tea, and we can have a nice visit."

"Hell, Mom, it's got to be eighty degrees out. It's too bloody hot for tea."

"Of course, you're right. Sorry. I have some soft drinks that are cold."

Ryan's anger grew. Now, he slammed the driver's door, hard. He regretted it when Lily jumped, then shot him a guilty look.

"Oh, how silly of me. John, I don't think you remember Ryan Kincaid...from next door. Ryan, this is my son, John."

"Hey."

Ryan nodded in response to the one word greeting. He turned to Lily. "You go ahead inside. I wouldn't mind a cup of tea myself. I'll unload the car."

"You're staying?" John gave him a cross look. "I have some private matters to discuss with my mother. Private family matters."

"You won't even know I'm around," Ryan's responded. No way in hell he'd leave Lily alone with this little pit viper. "Besides, I promised your mother that I'd be at her service as soon as we got home." When Lily shot him a wild-eyed look, he continued blandly. "Hooking up her computer, showing her how to work the digital camera, and setting up her cell phone for her."

For the first time, John let his gaze wander to the car. Several parcels covered the back seat. Ryan, however, walked straight to the trunk and opened it.

"Crap, Mom, what the hell did you just do? Blow all your money at the mall? If Grandma finds out, she's going to tear a strip off you for being such a spendthrift."

"Go on inside, honey. I'll be in as soon as I help Ryan unload the car."

"No, you go on." Ryan's tone gentled as he took in Lily's dejected expression. When she continued to look at him with uncertainty in her eyes, he gave her his best smile. "This will only take me a couple of trips. Go on and visit with your son."

If the little bugger had been his kid, first he'd have gotten a smack for the tone he'd used on his mother. *Then* he'd have been shown the door out, not the door in. But Lily's children were her business. He intended to do his damnedest not to interfere. A few bouts of sex didn't give him the right to voice an opinion on family. The day may come, but not today. As he gathered the first load to take into the house, he vowed to keep his cool.

It was a resolve doomed to failure.

Chapter 6

Lily felt her cheeks heat. She had never overspent in her life, yet her mother often censured her for it. The woman persisted in accusing her of being foolish, selfish, or a spendthrift. Eloise Robertson Riggs specialized in giving her account of Lily's many flaws in the presence of Lily's children.

Lily felt the joy and excitement of the day evaporate even as she realized that John would likely tell his grandmother about her shopping spree.

Determined to make the best of the situation, she offered her son a seat at the table. "How's your sister?"

"I don't know. Okay, I guess. We don't hang with the same crowd. I think I heard her mention something about wanting to go to Europe in August. Good luck, I say. Unless, of course, Dad isn't tightening the wallet on *her*. She's his favorite, so she might be able to swing it."

Lily frowned as the familiar sentiment of everyone-always-liked-her-best washed over her. She'd once believed, fervently, that when her son and daughter became adults, they would behave as adults toward each other. In her heart, she'd hoped they'd become friends. But it didn't appear to have happened so far. Lily acknowledged the stray thought that perhaps neither of them had reached adulthood, yet. Tramping down the unkind sentiment, she focused again on John.

"What about you? Any plans for the rest of the summer? Are you still thinking of getting your masters, or are you going to look for a position someplace, now?"

"What the hell is it with everyone, anyway? First Dad and now you. You're both so anxious for me to get working. I thought I made it clear, years ago, that I planned to go as far in my field as I could. With only a B.A.

in Social Work, I don't qualify for much more than being a teaching assistant at a university. I want an upscale practice, I want to write some books, maybe have a few lecture tours. To do that, I need my doctorate."

Accustomed to the tone, Lily didn't even take offense, though a headache began to form behind her eyes. "Yes, I know that's what you'd planned. But I didn't know if you'd changed your mind, or not. I didn't know if maybe you and Sheila planned—"

"Sheila's history. I blew her off a couple of months ago. We wanted different things. I'm too young to think about settling down, anyway. I haven't even had a chance to have any fun yet."

"Ah." Lily surmised that the break-up with his long time girlfriend pained him more than he wanted to admit. John had always been far more sensitive than he'd ever let on. She thought perhaps only she, of all the family, perceived this vulnerability in him.

"And anyway, the courses I'm taking are very intense. You couldn't possibly understand, because you never even *went* to university. It's damn hard work. I need the summer months to relax and decompress."

Lily fought down the tiny spurt of anger at the dig. "I know you do, John." She went to the fridge and surveyed the contents. The nagging headache in the back of her head grew. She hoped it wouldn't develop into full-blown pain.

"I've got cola and ginger ale," she offered, forcing a smile.

"Cola."

Knowing her son's preferences, she got down one of her nicest glasses, filled it with ice, then brought the glass and can to the table. Before sitting down, she put the kettle on.

Ryan came in from the car with the final load—the computer.

"Did you want this in the office?" he asked, and she knew he referred to the small downstairs room that Mark had set up as such, and that Lily had left the desk and chair in.

"Yes, please. Kettle's on. I'll call you when it's ready."

"Thanks, hon."

Lily shot a worried look at John. But he hadn't noticed the endearment, had in fact totally ignored Ryan, concentrating instead on pouring his drink.

"Poverty pop", he commented, setting the can aside. The term differentiated generic soft drinks from the brand-named products.

"You can't afford the real thing, but you go out and blow a fortune on yourself. Dad told me you made a mistake, moving all the way out here. From what I can see, you did."

"Excuse me? Your father said…what?"

"He worried you'd be here and no one could keep an eye on you, and I guess he knew what he was talking about."

Your father wasn't so concerned that he didn't stab me in the back during the divorce, Lily thought darkly. Instead, she said, "I'm sure you misunderstood. Your father has better things to do with his time than concern himself with me."

"The thing is, he's right. This is no place for you. Stuck out here in the boonies, no life to speak of. Well, I know you've never really had much of a life anyway, but still. Even *you* must get bored out of your mind way out here. You need to sell this place. I've been browsing on the Web. There are housing developments going up all around here. How big is the property? I bet you could net a cool couple of million out of a sale."

"I don't want to sell, John. I'm happy here."

"Yeah, it's all about you, isn't it? Always has been, just like Grandmother always says. You never gave a shit about us, Alice and me, just went about doing whatever the hell you wanted. Then you walked out on us and left us with Dad. Well, see, the thing is I need you to start doing your part here. Next year's tuition is due soon, and Dad's making noises that he wants me to move out of the house. Like, sure, I can do that if he wants to get me a place—a nice apartment in just the right area would be great. But no, he doesn't want to do that. He actually had the nerve to suggest I get a job. I can't work and study at the same time. But if you sold this place, then with my share of the money, I could manage just fine. Maybe even take a nice vacation. I've never had one of my own, you know."

The headache had advanced, and Lily sat back as the pounding took up a rhythm all on its own. Anger, hard to control, bubbled like lava through her veins. She put all her effort into choosing just the right words.

"I didn't 'walk out' on you and your sister, John. Your father asked for a divorce and *ordered* me to leave. You make it sound as if you and Alice are in grade school, instead of grad school."

"Whatever."

John didn't take correction well, never had. He'd just given Lily his version of events, and she knew from experience he would never be persuaded his version was wrong. The root of the problem never changed. John wasn't getting what he considered his 'fair share.' A tiny voice pulled big chunks of guilt out from hidden corners in her conscience. She *had* never worked outside the home, so she *had* never pulled down a paycheck, nor had she *personally* ever paid a penny toward his or his sister's education.

"I could probably manage to help you out with some money toward your tuition. If you're stuck for a place to live and have nowhere to go, well of course you could move in here. But I'm not selling my home, John."

"You can't possibly like living out here. It's barren!"

"I do like living out here. I've always loved it here." Lily understood the bottom line with her son, she always had. Reaching for her purse, she pulled out her checkbook.

"Will a hundred do for now?"

The look on his face told her he was insulted. The kettle chose that moment to break into a full whistling boil, and Lily got up and made the tea.

"A hundred? Give me a break. That just won't cut it, Mom. I have expenses. I need some new clothes. Hell, I shouldn't have to live like this."

"Well, I guess I could let you have five hundred right now," she said slowly. "If you need more for tuition, I'll have to make arrangements, and that will take time. So you'll have to let me know."

Lily had no doubt John would take the money, and in such a way as to make it seem a favor to her. She did know her son. Twenty-three years old, and she seriously doubted he would ever grow up. She understood, deep inside, the headache she currently suffered stemmed from being with the young man sitting across the table from her. The guilt of that knowledge increased the pounding.

"Well, it's better than nothing, I suppose. But you're going to have to do something, Mom. You're going to have to sell this place and contribute your fair share for a change. Dad's done it all by himself, all these years. It's time for you to step up to the plate."

* * * *

Ryan stayed put for a long moment after the back door slammed and her son started the Honda and left. It had taken more will than he could have imagined to not go marching into the kitchen and smack that little prick in the mouth. The computer had been unpacked, the components connected and plugged in. All that remained was to turn it on and show Lily how to use it. He should probably just stay there for a bit longer and let his temper simmer down.

Fuck that. Tossing the user's guide for the PC onto the desk, he headed for the kitchen.

Lily sat, elbows on the table, head in her hands. He opened his mouth, then closed it again, battling with himself. One half of him wanted to scream at her for taking the bullshit she'd just been served, the other half yearned to gather her close and soothe the hurt he knew she felt.

It took her a moment to realize he'd come into the room. When she finally looked up at him, he wanted to cringe at the battered expression she wore.

"Oh. Ryan. The tea. I'm sorry, I'll just—"

"Sit, babe, I'll get it."

"Thanks."

"You're welcome."

After pouring two cups of the beverage, Ryan set the mugs on the table, along with the sugar and cream. Then he sat down opposite her. He didn't say anything. He'd never been so pissed off, but he had to remember that he really didn't have the right to make judgments, or say anything negative about Lily's family.

"He's not a bad kid. He's just been under a lot of stress lately. His schooling, and the divorce." Lily's words sounded tired, and Ryan felt the steel of his resolve begin to melt. "The only thing is, I know he's going to call Mother and complain to her about how selfish I'm being. Which means she's either going to phone, or come out here, too. And that's one thing, right now, that I don't need. I'm going to have to have a look at my finances and see what I can swing for him and Alice. He's right. I need to assume my share of the expense for their educations."

Ryan's   none-of-my-business-not-going-to-open-my-mouth   policy shattered.

"He's a little piece of shit who needs his ass kicked from here into the next county for talking to you like he did."

"Ryan!"

"I'm sorry, babe. But somebody has to tell you the truth. He's what? Twenty-one? Twenty-two?"

"He's going to be twenty-four next month, but—"

"Fuck, at his age I'd already worked myself half way around the world. 'You're going to have to contribute your fair share for a change.' What bullshit. What complete and utter bullshit. Somebody needs to tell that punk the world doesn't revolve around him. You don't owe him a damn thing, Lily. Not anymore. He has to learn to make his own way, just like everybody else. It's way passed time he grew up."

"That's not fair. You don't understand. *He's my son.* Of course I have responsibilities toward him! Parenting isn't a job that ends when your kids turn twenty-one. It's a life-long commitment. I *will* admit he spoke a tad disrespectfully toward me just now. But he's a very sensitive young man. He's obviously worried about his future. If his father has cut off his spending money, or asked him to move out, it's only understandable—"

"He's your son, and your *responsibility* is to help him become a mature, self supporting, contributing member of society. Not to enable him to shirk responsibility and get a free ride in life. You think you're helping him out? Hell, Lily, you're crippling him!"

"You don't know anything about being a parent. How dare you say that to me!"

"I know about being a human being. I know about being a man. And I know that your son is a selfish, narcissistic little monster. It's easier to give in than to stand your ground, isn't it? Life is much easier if you avoid all those nasty confrontations. He wants you to be his mommy without allowing you to be his mother, and you do nothing to stop him."

"No one talks to me like that in my own house. Get out! Get out right now!"

"No one but relatives, apparently. I don't need to put up with this bullshit. I'm out of here."

* * * *

For the second time in a half hour, the kitchen door slammed. The last time, Lily felt relief. This time, she felt her heart breaking. It didn't matter that Ryan's words echoed her own guilty thoughts. The roar of a Harley screaming down the driveway seemed the last upset that she could bear. Lily's emotions felt ready to explode. Her head pounded, and the echo in her conscience that agreed with everything Ryan had just said butted up against her instincts to protect her child from attack. On top of everything she'd experienced these last few days, Ryan's condemnation of her really proved to be the last straw.

Laying her head down on the table, she surrendered as she rarely had in her life, as the sobs ravaged her.

Chapter 7

He owed her an apology.

That idea first whispered to him before his Harley had cleared her driveway. It had been easy to ignore the truth when it just muttered in the back of his mind. But now, several hours later, with the sun having set and the stars come out, that whisper became a roar.

He'd been angry on her behalf, so what, he turns around and beats up on her, too? He'd wanted to punch that kid in the nose, not bloody his mother's. He'd known the instant he'd stepped into that kitchen Lily was hurting.

He'd never believed in kicking people when they were down, and felt like the lowest kind of slug because he'd done just that to Lily. Which put him, he thought sourly, on the same level as her son.

What she said to him had been absolutely true. He had no experience being a parent. He'd lost his mother at the age of eleven, so he had no idea how she would have treated him as a teen or young man. But his father had always been on his side, no matter what. When Ryan had eschewed getting a steady job after university and yearned to travel the world, living his rebel-without-a-clue ideal, his dad had told him to go ahead and follow his dream. Then, travel-weary and a bit wiser, he'd returned home, only to be welcomed back with open arms. He'd been gone nearly a decade. Years when he should have been at home, helping his aging father with the farm. Years spent focusing on himself and ignoring—or neglecting—the man who had sired him.

So, he may not have ever lipped off the way John had today, but he'd been no sterling example of filial devotion, himself.

Ryan exhaled heavily as he looked across the field to Lily's place. He'd lied to himself. He'd convinced himself that her family relationships weren't any of his business. But he cared about her far more than he'd admitted to himself. They had more going for them than just sex. He didn't know what the future held for their relationship. But he'd asked her to trust him with her body, no holds barred. He'd shown her things today, painted a picture of a path that, if taken, would leave her more open and vulnerable than she'd ever been in her life. That was a hell of a lot to ask of a woman as inexperienced as Lily.

In return, he could at least stand with her. He didn't like the way her son had spoken to her, but she needed to be able to trust he wouldn't jump on the bandwagon of 'beating up on Lily.'

"Fuck." Straightening from his slouching position on the porch, Ryan could only hope that his apology wouldn't come too late.

The sudden flash of light in Lily's yard caught his attention. He watched as those lights made their way down her lane, turned toward him. When they slowed at the head of his own driveway, he held his breath.

As Lily's car crept down his driveway, he took the steps off his porch and went to meet her.

* * * *

She turned off the car, but didn't know what to do next. Her headlights had shown him waiting for her, but she simply couldn't move.

She'd spent the afternoon in tears, and reflection. Everything Ryan said echoed her deepest feelings. She'd envied him his freedom to speak those feelings even as she lashed out at him for it. Those emotions, the ones she'd never voiced, lived deep within her, wrapped in guilt. She'd had enough of the guilt. She hated the way her children treated her. John walked all over her, and Alice—well, Alice pretty much ignored her. Hell, she hated the way her *mother* treated her. But she didn't know how to make it all stop. The training, the inclinations, went way down, deep.

She hoped she could mend the hole she'd torn today in her relationship with the one person who had so quickly come to mean so very much to her.

Ryan strolled toward her, but instead of opening her door, he put his hands on the car, leaning toward the open window. She didn't know if that meant he didn't want her to get out of the car, or not. That he might damn near broke her heart. Still, she had to tell him what she'd decided to tell him. With only the sound of crickets disturbing the silence, her gaze rested on her hands as she searched for the right words.

"I'm sorry," she ventured quietly. "I'm sorry I lost my temper with you. That I told you to leave. Everything," she stopped for a moment when her breathing hitched, when tears coated her voice. Inhaling deeply, she forced back the lump taking over her throat and continued on. "Everything you said was right. More than right. It's what I've been thinking, feeling, for years. I *am* a coward. Far too cowardly to—"

Lily jumped when he yanked the door open.

He lifted her out and into his arms before she could draw another breath.

"No, babe. I'm the one who's sorry. I didn't have the right to say those things to you. I don't know what it's like to be a parent, but I know it's a job that never ends."

The breath from his apology brushed her hair, warming the skin of her neck and shoulder even as it warmed her chilled and battered heart.

"I want you to have the right to tell me anything and everything."

"There's that word again."

Lily knew tears weakened her laugh. When Ryan had hauled her into his arms, she began to cry.

She pulled back just enough that she could look into his eyes and cup his face in her hands.

"The way you saw me today, it's the way I've always been. They get that tone—every single member of my family can put on that tone—and something inside me shrivels. My thoughts may be slapping them back, but only my thoughts. And then I feel so guilty for even that much."

"You shouldn't feel guilty for wanting to be treated with respect, Lily. Everyone deserves to be treated with respect."

"I know that. In my head." She returned to the haven of Ryan's embrace. His arms enfolding her gave her the most comforting, the most secure feeling she had ever known.

"Please don't hate me because I'm a wimp. Don't turn away from me. I...I need you. And I want you."

"I could never hate you. And I've wanted you far too long to turn away from you now."

Lily felt the pressure of his hand on her head and lifted her mouth to his. His taste, already so familiar to her, soothed. Each time his mouth mated with hers felt as new and exciting as the first time. The void that had ripped open in her when she thought she'd lost him flooded with need, hot piercing need that fired her blood and sparked her senses. Surrendering completely to him, she wound her arms around his neck and climbed him. When her legs encircled his waist, when she felt the denim-covered ridge of his engorged penis push against the folds of her pussy, she melted.

"You didn't put on any panties."

"No," she said and then, "Hurry!" when she felt his hand brush her mound and knew the movements meant he was freeing his cock from his pants.

"Hang on to me. Just let me protect..."

"Ryan!"

His words sounded strained and she wondered if he'd ever get that condom on. Finally, Lily sighed mightily as Ryan pushed his flesh into her. Then she just held on, the exquisite thrusting of his cock in and out of her, the most delicious feeling she'd ever known. He cursed, but Lily didn't mind, for she knew that the fever burning hotly inside her raged in him as well.

Her groans turned to pleas, and then a scream of completion as the orgasm rippled and bubbled, erupting from the exact place where his pubic hair rubbed her clitoris, a pyroclastic flow of climax to every one of her nerve endings.

"Let me drive you back home, Lily. Let me stay the night."

"Yes."

* * * *

As soon as she got out of the car, Ryan scooped her into his arms and began stripping her. Lily wanted to help, but his urgently whispered, "Let me," stilled her hands and sped her heart. He stripped her quickly, setting her on her feet only long enough to whip off his own clothes.

"Hold your breath."

That was the only warning she got before he lifted her and stepped into the deep end of the pool. They sank quickly. Lily hung onto Ryan, and could feel when his legs hit the bottom and he pushed up powerfully. When they broke the surface, she sputtered and coughed, and laughed.

"Are you crazy?"

His laughter fed music into the night. "Certifiably."

Even as she shivered, he pulled her closer. "I had plans, things I wanted to do with you—to you. Those plans haven't changed. But if after the way I behaved this afternoon, you no longer trust me to—"

"I trust you." When he continued to look at her, she stretched up and placed a gentle kiss on his lips. "I do." Naked, wet, and plastered against this virile man had become Lily's favorite state of existence.

And maybe, she thought, the time had come for her to dare, just a little.

"Being like this, with you, makes me feel free. For the first time in my life I know that here, I can be selfish, and it's all right. Here, I can put aside the walls and barriers that I realize I've always kept between myself and everyone else."

"Thank God for those walls, Lily. I have a feeling that if you hadn't learned to develop them—likely early on in life—that bastard ex of yours might have killed your spirit completely."

"Maybe. But those walls have kept me very alone, too, Ryan. They prevented me from making any friends, having any kind of a real life. That's how I know they're gone, with you. Because I feel free, and on the verge of *having* a life. Remember how I wondered what I should do—if I should work?"

"Yes."

"Maybe it's not a question of doing, at this point in my life. I really don't have to work, or make money. So maybe it's not a case of doing. Maybe...maybe it's a case of *evolving. Of becoming.* Maybe that's why I've been given this second chance. Maybe that's why I've been given you."

"What do you want to become, Lily?"

"Stronger. Freer. I want to be...God, I want to be not only self aware, but *self-assured.* I want to walk down the street with my head held high. I want to take a stand and not falter. I want to enjoy every single minute of every single day and know at the end that I did what I wanted, and that I have no regrets."

"You want to live."

"Hell, yes, I want to live. For the first time in my life, I want to live."

"And you think that being with me, like this, will give you all that?"

"I know it will. Because it's already begun to. Before you, I never would have had the courage to look a man in the eye and tell him I want him. I want you, Ryan. Every single way I can have you." The look in his eyes melted her heart and stirred her blood. She didn't think she'd ever get tired of looking at him, kissing him, fucking him. At least she hoped not, as she swallowed a giggle at how easily her mind had thought about fucking.

"You humble me, Lily. From the first moment, you've meant more to me than just sex. Fucking you meant the realization of a thirteen-year-old dream. And even then, it meant more. I don't know where to start."

His voice, a bass rumble, vibrated low in her belly. She felt her smile widen slowly and thought that, in time, she just might be able to do anything. "That's easy," she said, her own thoughts and words spiking her arousal. "I seem to recall mention of a feast."

Chapter 8

"Are you going to let me have you?'

"Pardon me, but didn't you just have me in your driveway not half an hour ago?"

"Mmm, but what about now? And in having you now what I want is for you to surrender to me completely." He stroked his hands down her body, smoothing soap along her fine lines and lush curves. Steam from the shower enveloped them in a sensual mist, the warm water caressing them both. He'd talked her into showering together to rinse away the chlorine from the pool. But more, he wanted another chance to have his hands on her. He loved the feel of her skin. Her flesh felt soft all over, but other women had been soft. She responded so hotly to his touch, but other women had done the same. He couldn't say why Lily seemed different, better, *more* than any woman he'd ever had. He only knew that she was all of those things.

Mine. He'd never been a man to feel possessive of a woman. But that single possessive pronoun had shouted itself to Ryan the first instant his body merged with hers. That sense of fit, that sense of rightness hadn't diminished one whit, and he had the suspicious feeling that it wouldn't for a very long time to come, if ever.

"Well?" he asked, quite aware that Lily hadn't answered him. But neither had her body become tense under his hands, so he guessed she didn't feel threatened by his request.

"Surrender…what?"

Ryan chuckled, and pulled her flush against his front, his hands sliding up her belly to cup plump wet breasts. Smiling when she hissed in pleasure, he plunged his tongue into her ear. Then whispered the one word guaranteed to make her shiver. "Everything."

He felt it then, a slight tremble that shuddered through her. Whether from arousal, or trepidation, he didn't know. Arousal could be plumbed from a pool of trepidation. Not that he wanted to terrify her, but a little healthy suspense wouldn't necessarily go amiss.

Since they'd played back and forth with that word all day, Ryan decided to give her an example.

"I want to begin by shaving you."

"I shaved in the shower this morning."

Ryan smiled. While one hand squeezed a breast, the other wandered down over her belly and combed through the short auburn curls that covered her mons.

"I meant here, darling."

"Oh. Um…I've heard that when it grows back, it itches."

"I'll just have to make sure that it doesn't grow back then, won't I?"

"Oh."

Ryan nibbled her ear, squeezed the breast he held, and plunged two fingers into her. Working them quickly, he used his thumb to stroke her clit.

"Say yes, Lily. Surrender to me. Completely."

"Ryan!"

He held her off from orgasm by changing the rhythm of his fingers. When she whimpered, he stopped completely.

"Yes! All right!"

"Mine, to do with as I please?" One little caress accompanied his question.

"Yes!"

Satisfied, Ryan bent her forward, her curved and lovely ass right in front of him. Reaching onto the shower shelf, he snagged the foil packet he'd set there earlier. When he had prepared himself, he slowly rubbed his penis against her wet folds. He could feel her pussy throbbing with arousal. He plunged his cock into her, hard and fast and deep. When she came, he let himself come with her.

* * * *

She couldn't stop the shivering that had overtaken her. She didn't feel afraid. Well, not much. Being spread out on her bed, blindfolded, a little fear was understandable. She had asked him to show her everything, but she'd had no idea what 'everything' encompassed. He'd asked her to surrender to him completely, and she had said yes. She might not know the details of what would happen next, but she knew that she trusted him. Incredibly, she trusted him, as she had no one else.

The sensation of wetness, and the drag of steel brought her back to the here and now. She didn't even shave her 'bikini line.'

She'd never imagined shaving her pubis, never really thought about it, except for the impression buried down deep, just now surfacing: *Only bad girls shaved down there.*

Her hand didn't wield the razor, though. Her lover's did. So what did that make her? A very bad girl? In the next heartbeat, with the next cold glide of the razor over her labia, she knew what it made her. It made her free.

Somehow, her emotions linked the act of shedding the hair that society expected her to wear with the shedding of the roles and responses that had bound her all her life.

In reality, freedom more than liberated. It terrified. Everything changed. Everything became new and different for her now. The rules and traditions that had held her in place, ground her down, had been obliterated, banished the moment she'd said yes to Ryan's provocative demand.

What she had surrendered to him, totally, wasn't her will, but her past.

Another slow, meticulous stroke of the blade, and cool air wafted across where she was nude for the first time since puberty. He had ordered her to keep her knees bent and legs spread so that he could work freely. Those legs trembled now from the force of keeping them that way.

"Almost done, Lily. Hold still, sweetheart. I don't want to have to tie your legs apart. At least…not tonight."

Lily moaned as another shiver coursed over her. Had she really believed herself to be cold, asexual? Ryan could render her close to orgasm with a single daring sentence. His deep, sexy chuckle just added to the heat consuming her from within. She'd already come twice tonight. Unbelievable, really, when she'd had so few orgasms in her life before this intriguing younger man rode into it.

"There. Now, just lay still. Relax your legs, but leave them spread for me, babe. I'm going to go get a warm, wet cloth and rinse you off."

It seemed to take him forever, but he returned and cleaned her.

"Do you know what the best thing is about digital cameras, Lily?"

The non sequitur confused her. Until she heard the first ominous *whirr* and *click*. As awareness came, she moved her arms, instinctively seeking to cover herself.

"No, Lily. It's your camera. This is just for the two of us. Trust me."

Slowly, she returned her arms to where they'd been spread out wide. She heard a couple of more clicks, and then the sound of the camera being set aside.

"Okay, I'm going to put a few drops of oil on you, now. Where it lands, I want you to use your hands and slowly massage it in."

Lily nearly yelped as something warm and wet landed with a little plop on her belly. The tangy-sweet aroma of strawberries filled the air and she inhaled deeply. Her mouth watered in response to the fruity smell. She licked her lips and swallowed as she recalled Ryan's promise of a strawberry feast.

More drops fell, this time on her breasts, and she moved her hands to caress and smooth.

"Your nipples are hard, baby. You're turned on. Pinch them for me."

A moan escaped her as she obeyed, and shafts of pleasure speared from her breasts to her pussy. It felt almost as good as when he pinched them. Her hips twitched and she clenched her inner muscles in response to the arousal.

"Good girl. More, now."

The liquid landed low on her belly and she dipped her fingers in, spreading it around her navel, to the edges of her hips, and just above her mons. It felt wonderful, this massaging, and she wondered that she'd never dared such a private rite before. She shivered. Her flesh pebbled, breast to thighs.

Oil landed on her mound and began to trickle down to the folds of her vagina.

Her right hand moved down to cover and stroke, to rub and tease. She felt moisture gathering inside her and began to work her hips in counter point to her busy fingers, feeding the flames.

"Yeah, play with your slit for me, Lily. It turns me on to see you play with yourself like that. Use both hands, babe. Rub your hungry little pussy with both hands. But don't come, honey. Don't come yet."

When more of the liquid landed on her, she gave a primal sound of need and pleasured herself even more. It no longer mattered that Ryan might be snapping pictures of her. It certainly didn't matter if she gave him one hell of a show. She turned him on, turned herself on, and that was all that mattered.

"Slide a finger into your pussy, babe. Let me see you finger-fuck yourself."

Lily had never done this before. That one time she'd masturbated, it had been a simple matter of picturing a naked sixteen-year-old Ryan and rubbing her clit. She'd come in moments, then, and had felt so guilty for touching herself in such a *naughty* way.

Her finger encountered a hot, wet tunnel that eagerly sucked the digit down to the knuckle. When Ryan murmured for her to add a second, and then a third finger, she did so without thinking, only striving to please them both.

"Come for me, Lily."

"Ah, Ryan!" his name emerged as a sob on her lips as she tipped over the edge. Her body curved up, a tight bow of tension, her thumb stroking her own clit as she came and came. Exhausted, she fell back on the pillows, her hands sprawled out to the side, her entire body lax.

In the next instant, she felt Ryan's mouth on her.

* * * *

"I can't."

"You can," Ryan said as he nestled his face into her moisture. "You will." He closed his mouth over her clit and sucked rhythmically, his hands holding her hips in place when she squirmed. Because he knew she would be tender, he let the tiny nubbin of flesh slip out of his mouth. He kissed and lapped at her thighs, giving her a few moments to rest, to let the rawness he knew she must have been feeling, ease.

"I can taste strawberries and your own particular nectar. Very intoxicating."

He smiled when she whimpered, and he continued to kiss and caress her legs, her thighs, her belly. He avoided her pussy, waiting until he heard her breathing hitch, until he knew that she could take more.

He returned his mouth to her then, holding his lips open, rubbing them back and forth slowly across her slit. Aroused, her labia thickened and opened. He pulled back, blew cool breath on her wet flesh, and chuckled when she shivered. Using his tongue, he traced every centimeter of her pussy, lapping, teasing, and then using his open mouth to give her big, sucking kisses. Releasing her hips now that she moved with him and not against him, he reached up to fondle pretty coral-tipped breasts. His own arousal burned, a molten river heating his blood, engorging his cock. He rubbed his condom-covered shaft lightly against the bed sheet, and knew it wouldn't take much for him to come. But tasting her, teasing and arousing her added another layer of seduction, one that gave him a deep pleasure the like of which he'd never known.

Of course, he could fuck her another way. Squeezing her nipples tightly, he thrust his tongue into her.

"Oh, God."

He smiled but kept up his assault, lapping and sucking and thrusting with his tongue and lips, petting and caressing with his hands. His cock, rock hard, needed to plow into her soon, but he wanted to give her just a little more first. And take a little more for himself, as well. He'd never been so turned on in his life.

When the sound of Lily's moans became frantic, he pulled his left hand away from her breast and trailed it down her body.

Two fingers shot into her opening, caressing the top of her canal, finding the tiny button of hardness within, that some thought didn't exist. He tickled her G-spot with quick little strokes as he again sucked on her clit.

The grab of her fingers at his hair, the tension of her body, the ear-piercing scream and release of nectar into his hungry mouth told him her orgasm whipped fiercely through her.

He climbed up her prone and panting form and thrust his cock into her, burying himself to the hilt in one solid push. Whipping the blindfold off her, he kissed her, a deep tonsil-tickling, flavor-sharing kiss as he pumped toward ejaculation. Wilder and hotter than anything he'd ever experienced, he wondered, when the climax came, if he would ever get enough of her.

For a long time, they lay tangled together, gasping, shivering, as the aftermath of explosive orgasmic sex washed through them.

"I have the feeling," Lily said at last, "that *everything* just might kill me."

"Darling," Ryan replied softly as he rolled to his side and gathered her close, "we've barely scratched the surface of *everything*."

Chapter 9

The old broad had been pitifully easy.

John poured himself a snifter of his father's best brandy, and reviewed this evening's performance—at least Act One of it. He'd shown up at his grandmother's door with flowers. He'd carried himself just right, and before long, she asked him what troubled him. Putting on a brave front, he of course denied any problems. His grandmother could be counted on to act like a bull terrier when she got a notion in her head, and he'd enjoyed his role immensely. Finally he confessed his deep concern for his poor, witless mother, spending so freely, isolated in the middle of nowhere, nobody to guide her. Hinting—oh just lightly hinting—about the 'much younger man' who seemed quite at home in his mother's house. Then he'd delivered the clincher. How unfair that his mother possessed such a large, unused, and lucrative parcel of land when her children needed financial support and assistance.

He wouldn't be surprised if dear old granny made a beeline for the farm the very next day. Though, of course, he knew his grandmother better than that. She wouldn't set foot on the place. At least not until she'd made a few harassing phone calls, first.

His grandfather, he figured, hadn't died of heart problems. The poor old bastard had likely seen death as his only escape.

The sound of the front door opening alerted him that his father and the bimbo had arrived home. Now it was time for Act Two. Before long, that wretched farm would be sold. He figured his share would be more than enough to set up his own apartment, pay for the rest of his education, with plenty left over to live a few years in style.

* * * *

"John. You missed dinner. Mary's mother was disappointed." Reginald Martin came into the den, walking directly to the bar where he poured his own after-dinner drink.

"Sorry about that, Dad. I'd been out to visit Mom, then...well, I had to go see Grandmother, too."

"Your mother is well, I trust."

John hesitated before answering. "I suppose. I didn't stay long. She had...company, and I'm afraid I felt very much 'de trop,' if you know what I mean."

"Oh?"

John knew he had his father's full attention now.

"No, I probably just read the situation wrong. She claimed the guy lived next door, and just came to hook up her new computer. He seemed very young—I don't think he was my age...yeah, she's probably just helping the guy out, paying him to do stuff for her around the place or something. Lots of younger men call older women 'honey.' Doesn't mean they're like...a couple...or anything."

"It's kind of you to be concerned about your mother, under the circumstances. I don't know why she insisted on moving out to that backwater. Your grandmother, I'm certain, expressed her unhappiness with the fact."

"I thought Mother might have been, you know, maybe prepping the place for resale. There are some pretty high-end housing developments in the area. I checked. The land she's sitting on has to be worth a bloody fortune. I told her she should look into selling it. After all, both Alice and I have a few more years of university to pay for and it's only right she contribute her fair share, give you a bit of a break."

"That would be a good idea," Reg agreed.

John could see his father was thinking, and thinking hard. His work, for the moment, was done.

"Yeah, well she shot that idea down real fast." Then he checked his watch. "I think I'll head up. Good night, Dad."

John knew he'd pushed all the right buttons. It only remained for him to sit back and wait for things to happen.

* * * *

Lily dusted her hands off and stood back. The somewhat battered desk had been hiding in a corner of the barn, covered with a tarp. She didn't know if the piece was an antique, or not. Constructed of solid wood, it had definitely seen better days. Not ten feet away from where the desk had been stored sat another piece of furniture. At first she took it for a mini china cabinet, owing to the presence of doors missing their glass. But when she examined both pieces again, she realized that the second piece fastened on top of the first.

She tried to remember whether or not the desk appeared in any of the old family photographs her uncle had. But she wasn't as familiar with the photos as she might have been. Her mother—her uncle's sister—hadn't kept any photos of her life as a child on the farm. There'd been a falling out at some point between her mother and the rest of the Robertson clan. Lily never did learn what it had been about. She decided to look through the photos later to see if this piece of furniture played any role in family history.

In the meantime, she needed to have this piece appraised.

Why?

Lily shuddered involuntarily as the question reverberated in her mind. She tilted her head and looked at the forgotten desk. Thinking in terms of dollars and cents emulated her mother's thinking. And her ex-husband's. But did she want to think that way? Really?

She liked the look of the desk. Couldn't that be enough? Her living room, sparsely furnished as it was at the moment, needed more furniture. This desk, cleaned up, would look good in the corner, between the two windows. She wondered how expensive it would be to have the desk restored. It probably wouldn't cost that much. She could look in the yellow pages, find a cabinetmaker that took in pieces to refinish.

Or she could do the work herself.

No. She didn't know anything about restoring furniture. It would likely be hard, and possibly grimy work. She'd likely ruin her manicure, probably get slivers, and had no guarantee at all that she'd succeed.

And that, Lily thought with some resentment, sounded like her mother's thinking again. So *what* if restoration proved hard and grimy work? She'd never shied away from hard work. So what if she didn't achieve professional results? The piece would only be in her living room, not on exhibition somewhere.

Lily reached out and gently caressed the wood. It felt warm and vital under her hand. No, she didn't know anything at all about restoring furniture, but she bet she could find out how to do it, if she only investigated.

Turning sharply on her heel, she marched into the house, straight to her office. Switching on the computer, she settled herself comfortably in her chair and prepared to breech two personal horizons: Internet research and furniture re-finishing.

* * * *

"Grr. All right. Let me try this again."

"Who's winning?"

Lily turned at the sound of Ryan's voice and gave him a smile. She hadn't heard him come into the house, but she smiled, happy to see him. And standing there with a cocky grin and his arms akimbo, wasn't he one handsome son-of-a-gun?

"At the moment the machine is, but I hope to conquer it soon."

"Whatcha doing?"

"Trying to find out how to refinish furniture."

Rather than take over the task, Ryan pulled up a chair and sat beside her. Echoes from the past—a series of "Here, let me do that, you'll only mess it up/do it wrong/hurt yourself/look like a fool,"—skittered through her mind. Ryan knew very well she had no experience at this new medium. Since he made his living, and a pretty good one from what she could tell, using the computer, he likely excelled in its use. But he obviously had no need to show that skill off for her now, or to take control of her project.

She looked over at him, one eyebrow raised in question of what he thought of her efforts so far.

"You're doing all right."

"Yeah, now. The first thing I did was to query the keyword 'Furniture.' The machine promptly served me page one of twenty-seven million, four hundred thousand."

Ryan laughed. "You have to learn somehow. May I ask why furniture refinishing?"

"I found this old desk out in the barn. I thought if I could clean it up...anyway, it's a secretary desk, I've already figured that much out. It'll look something like this when it's done." She handed him a picture she'd managed to print of a desk that resembled the one in her barn.

"That would look good in the living room, between the windows."

Lily gave him a huge smile. "That's what I thought."

When he made no other comment, she totally relaxed. Since he hadn't voiced any reasons why she shouldn't pursue this particular endeavor, she felt free to discuss the matter openly. "I may get into it and find I don't like doing it."

"Then you can hire someone to finish it. Or, you may find it's an enjoyable hobby. You'll never know until you try."

She would never know until she tried. Impulsively, she framed his face with her hands and kissed him.

"Why did you do that?"

"Because I felt like it."

"Well, in that case."

Lily giggled as Ryan scooped her up and brought her to the floor, raining kisses all over her face. She laughed harder as he tickled her and undressed her at the same time. She helped him shed his own clothes, seeking to brand him with her mouth.

When he put his hands on her, when he cupped and squeezed her breasts, she stopped laughing and grabbed his hair and hauled him down for another kiss. Her gaze met his, and she saw the wonder there.

"I shouldn't want you again. We fucked all night long, and into the morning. I should be spent. But I do want you again, and I'm beginning to think I'll never have enough of you."

Ryan's words brought a lump to her throat. "I feel the same way. I never knew I could feel the way you make me feel."

"How do I make you feel?"

"Hot. Beautiful. Free. Like I really matter."

"You're all of those things, Lily. All of those things, and more."

"Kiss me like you mean it. Then make love to me."

* * * *

He'd told her no less than the truth. The lady not only epitomized heat and beauty, her presence in his life had become *vital*. The thought didn't scare him, not in the least. He didn't know if what they had between them would last a lifetime, or not. But he wanted, more and more, to find out if it could be so.

He kissed her, deeply, carnally, her flavor seeping into him. He touched and caressed where it pleased him to, and felt his own arousal kick higher as she gasped and writhed. He cherished her, with slow sipping kisses and long, tender strokes.

"I need you inside me."

"You're getting bolder," he replied, "I like that."

He handed her the condom package, let her slide the latex on him. Her touch nearly drove him over the edge. His hard cock hungered, so he let it feed on her, with a slow and thorough stroking in and out that thrilled them both. She fit him like a hot wet velvet glove.

"Squeeze me."

"Like this?"

She clenched her inner muscles gently, and he felt the caress down the length of his shaft. "Oh, yeah. Just like that."

He kissed her again, the thrusting both above and below in perfect cadence. When she wound her legs around his hips, he used a hand to lift her bottom even more tightly to him.

Sharp and needy replaced slow and thorough. No room here for words or wasted breath, there existed only the drive for more and still more. Mating evolved into a race with no quarter given, with the sweetest of rewards at the end. Hands clasped and fingers twined as hearts pounded and pleasure poured.

"I keep thinking it can't get better. Then it does."

Ryan gathered her close as he rolled to his side, her words fitting perfectly into the afterglow. Gradually, he became aware that the short fibers of the carpet prickled.

"Let's go upstairs."

"Good idea. If the object is to get us into bed for a nap first."

"I like the way you think, woman."

Getting to his feet, he helped Lily up and into another embrace, kissing her lightly. She reached to gather the clothes scattered on the rug just as the phone rang.

"I'll get the clothes. You get the phone."

A portable phone lay on the table beside the computer, and Ryan watched as Lily answered it. Her face tensed, and her expression drooped.

"Mother. Hello."

Ryan guessed it would be a bit awkward for a woman to chat with her mom while standing naked and freshly ravished by a lover. But as he continued to watch, as Lily's face filled with color and shame, he had to wonder about the woman on the other end of the line. And then that woman spoke, and though a half a room separated him from Lily, he could hear the shrill voice perfectly.

"Well, you've certainly done it this time, haven't you?"

Chapter 10

"How are you, Mother?"

"As if you care. I blame your father for this. He insisted you be named Lily. If I'd called you Maude, like *I* wanted, you'd be a much more sober and responsible daughter."

Lily closed her eyes as the familiar refrains of a lifetime began to play in her ear.

"Mother, could you tell me what it is I've done to upset you this time?"

Lily hadn't noticed that Ryan had left the room and then returned. But he must have, for he'd put his jeans back on and had brought her bathrobe to her. She shot him a grateful smile, and with his help, put the garment on. Covered, she immediately felt better.

"Don't sass, Lily. I *thought* we had agreed that it would be foolish and irresponsible to live in that falling-down shack out in that backwater township. I *thought* you agreed to do the sensible and responsible thing and unload that millstone your uncle saddled you with. That's how we left things when we spoke last month. I remember it perfectly well. What I would like to know is why you've gone against my wishes, and our agreement in this matter."

"Actually, Mother, that was just your thinking."

"Which, I recall succinctly, you didn't contradict."

"Because it would have been pointless. You don't want to know what I think, so I generally keep my thoughts to myself. You know I've always loved it here." Lily wasn't surprised when, predictably, her mother ignored that response and plowed on with her complaints.

"It's not enough that you've abandoned your children, physically. Now you've decided to abandon them financially, as well. And to completely ignore my wishes. Well, you've always been a thoughtless daughter."

Lily closed her eyes and rubbed her forehead. She was so very tired of hearing her mother's skewed interpretations of reality. "I've done no such thing. Reg asked for a divorce and insisted on keeping the house. Neither John nor Alice wanted to come with me, though I invited both to do so. Since they are both adults, fully grown, they had the right to choose to stay with Reg."

"And that's not the only thing I'm upset about. It's not even the worst of what you've done this time, as you well know. I expected better of you, Lily. Despite the fact that you've been a constant disappointment to me, I never would have expected you to do such a thing. You've sunk lower than even I could ever have guessed you would. John tells me you have a *boy* living with you. A boy young enough to be your *son*. Have you no *shame*? I can just imagine all the sinful goings on out there where there's no one who can see what you're up to."

Lily felt her face redden. She couldn't even say if her heightened color came from embarrassment or anger. "If John told you that, Mother, he lied. I certainly do not have anyone living with me, much less a boy." *That* remark, her mother apparently heard.

"How dare you call my sweet grandson a liar? Oh, it's just like you to try and deflect attention away from yourself, to blame everyone else for your own shortcomings. Well, if you think I'm going to sit idly by and allow you to make a laughing stock of yourself, or besmirch my good name and my position in the community by behaving in a wanton, brazen, *shameful* way, you can think again, missy. You leave me no choice. I'm going to call Reginald. Together, we'll just see what can be done about you. Make no mistake. You've gone too far this time!"

Lily held the receiver, the dial tone screaming after her mother's abrupt disconnect.

"Well, what a pleasant conversation." Lily carefully set her phone down. It wasn't until she looked up at Ryan that she realized he'd heard every word.

"I can't believe what I just heard. That was your *mother*?"

"Yes. She calls and berates, and I make noises till she's done. "

"She does that a lot, does she?"

"More in the past, before the kids grew up. If one of them didn't get what they wanted, I could be sure to hear from her. I can't prove it, but I've always had the impression that she would speak against me to them. Trash talk me, if you know what I mean."

Lily watched as Ryan shook his head. Amazing, how well she knew him, already. He wanted to give her his opinion, yet he recalled the fight they'd gotten into over his reaction to John. She thought that maybe this time, they could avoid a fight.

"I can't explain why it is I can think of a thousand and one things to say to her after the fact, yet remain virtually speechless in the heat of the moment. I just feel this…powerlessness come over me when confronted by her. I always have, all my life."

"She treated you like that when you were a kid?"

"Oh, yeah. I think my marriage to Reg is the only thing I ever did that pleased her. My faults, according to her, included laziness, eagerness to get my hands dirty like a common farmer, being not pretty enough, not graceful enough. But her favorites remained my selfishness, and my insistence on blaming everyone else for my numerous failures. Where she got those two from, I have no idea, because I have never been guilty of either. I'm sorry, Ryan. I'm sorry that you had to not only witness her vitriol, but my…passivity."

"Considering the nastiness of her attack, I think you handled her about the best way you could."

Lily walked over, and put her arms around Ryan.

"Thank you for saying that. For not pointing out that I'm a wimp."

"I don't think you're a wimp."

Lily kissed his mouth, taking him deep, her tongue dipping and playing with his. She loved the flavors of him, the way his hands caressed her back and bottom while his tongue danced with hers. She loved the way he made her feel sexy and attractive and *wanted*.

"Do you know what I want to do right now?" he asked her.

She adored the little half smile that teased his lips, and the twinkle in his eyes. "Play cribbage?" she suggested.

"Don't know how to play cribbage. No, I want to go to bed with you. I want to make love with you, and fall asleep with you in my arms. And I don't care if we get out of bed again before morning, or not."

"What an amazing coincidence."

Lily followed as he took her hand and led her to the bedroom. He shucked his jeans, reached for a condom, slipped it on his already hard cock. When he turned to her, when he pulled the belt of her robe, opening it, such hunger gleamed in his eyes she thought she knew what would come next. But he surprised her, yet again.

His hands trembled ever so slightly, she could feel them as he swept the robe from her, as he stroked her arms, her neck. He cupped her face, and she went up on her toes to close the distance between them. His kiss, soft, questing and, she thought, reverent, thrilled her. No one had ever kissed her like that. No one had ever treated her as if she was precious.

He sat on the bed and pulled her between his legs. Looking down at his head as he leaned forward to lick and kiss her breasts, her heart filled with such...love.

His brown hair glistened, so soft and long, she was tempted to run her fingers through it. He suckled and she arched, giving him freer access. Giving him everything.

Then he scooped her, laid her down, and took her mouth. The light, wet slide of lips, the gentle forays of his tongue seduced her completely. Her hand caressed his face, a touch of tenderness that he returned by bringing her hand to his lips and kissing it.

His mouth explored her then, slowly, patiently, and Lily thought she might go mad with his ministrations. She never knew the inside of her elbow to be an erogenous zone. Ryan's lips and tongue tasted her there, and her arousal grew. He traveled the length of one arm, then the other, stopping now and then to return to her lips. She reached for him, but he intercepted her hands, kissed them again.

"Just let me love you."

How could she resist? His lavish strokes, his deep kisses overwhelmed her. He nuzzled her breasts, then followed a line down, over her belly. Her body tensed as he neared her pussy, and she arched, her hips trying to entice him to settle there, to taste and tongue and tease.

But Ryan refused to be rushed, and just gave her eager mons a light stroke in passing, as he continued on. He kissed and licked her knees and nibbled her toes, and Lily ceased to think, she could only feel. Emotion and arousal became twined together in a silken cord that held her completely captive. When his hands urged her, she turned, and offered him her back.

The tiny dip in her spine, right at the top of her ass, proved a hot spot that reveled in Ryan's caresses. Her legs parted eagerly for him and when he suckled the dimples where bottom met thighs, she groaned. Her eyes closed and she could only surrender to the slow heavy beat of arousal that coursed through her. Her body moved and undulated following Ryan's worshipping mouth.

"*Please!*" The word escaped her when she feared she couldn't take any more. He urged her to turn over once more and her legs spread wide, waiting, before she had completed her turn. She wanted to reach down and stroke his ready cock, but he kissed her hand again even as he finally, finally thrust into her.

Lily lost touch with reality as her orgasm overpowered her. The spasms were long, electric, exciting, and she wrapped herself around him, arms and legs, pussy clinging to that wondrous cock as it moved in slow, measured beats in and out. Even when she felt his cock begin to twitch, even when she knew he came, Ryan's movement stayed slow and sure.

Rapture evolved into lassitude, and Lily cradled him close. He'd not said the words, but Lily felt the power of Ryan's love as a healing balm over her bruised spirit.

She continued to hold him close, the words not easily coming to her, either, and settled down to sleep.

But sleep eluded her, and long into the night the sentiment, if not the words, of what her mother had hurled her way began to gnaw on her conscience. She wished herself to be strong enough, grounded enough, to claim that she didn't care if anyone laughed at her for being a middle aged woman with a lover more than a decade her junior.

She wanted to be so carefree, but very much feared that she wasn't.

* * * *

Of all the people Lily thought she might encounter in a building supply store, her daughter wasn't one of them. She had just finished speaking with a clerk who had gone over the steps to strip and refinish furniture with her. She turned around, and spotted Alice.

"Mom!"

"Hi, honey." Lily didn't care if it did embarrass Alice. She gave her a hug anyway. And discovered, with some surprise, her hug returned shyly.

"Looks like you're getting ready to do something."

Lily followed Alice's gaze to her full cart.

"Yes. Believe it or not, I am about to try my hand at furniture refinishing. Ah…what brings you here?"

Alice pointed to another young woman talking to a clerk in the paint department. "Helping Julie pick out some paint. She's just moved into her own place and I promised I'd help her redecorate."

Lily watched the hesitant expression cross her daughter's face. She didn't have to wait long to find her thoughts.

"So…John says you're selling the farm and gonna be a millionaire."

Going on instinct, Lily replied, "He told me you're off to Europe in August."

"Where the hell did he get that idea?"

"Likely the same place he got the idea I'd sell my home. He actually suggested I do so the other day when he came to visit. But I told him I wasn't going to. And I'm not."

"Good. Don't let him push you into doing something you don't want to do."

Alice's attitude toward her brother had always been one Lily had classed as 'sibling rivalry.' To Lily, for the longest time now, Alice had seemed silent and sullen. But right this moment, having the most open conversation with her daughter that she'd had in a long time, Lily wondered if Alice's attitude in the past had reflected more than just her own brattiness.

"Listen...why don't you come out and have lunch with me next week? See the place?"

"I'd like that, mom."

Lily left the store with a smile on her face nearly big enough to drown the niggling worry that she'd awakened with.

* * * *

Ryan stood just outside the wide-opened doors of the barn, two tall glasses of lemonade in hand, and just watched as Lily worked. While he'd been at home most of the morning, finessing his latest program, she'd gone to town and purchased all the materials she needed to refinish the old desk she'd uncovered.

He'd been struggling with the anger that still seethed as a result of overhearing the phone call from her mother yesterday, and the lady herself had simply moved on. Though she had seemed a bit self-conscious, he reflected, first thing when they'd awakened in each other's arms just before dawn. He couldn't hold back the smile that slid across his face, recalling how he'd dealt with *that* emotion. By the time he thrust into her, she'd grabbed his hair in both fists and demanded he take her harder.

The strong smell of furniture stripper assaulted him, bringing him back to the present.

"Are you at a point where you can take a break?"

"Just a bit more of this noxious substance spread and…yeah."

She'd continued to coat the desktop as she'd spoken. When she dropped the brush back into the old coffee can, she stepped back and removed her gloves.

"I have about twenty minutes while the stripper soaks into the wood."

"Come on over to the picnic table and get out of these fumes."

"My plan, exactly."

Ryan waited until they sat facing each other at the picnic table before handing Lily the glass of lemonade. When she didn't look him in the eye, he sat back for a moment, assessing her.

"You seem to be coming along with that," he said, watching her.

"It's not as hard as I thought it might be. I read over the instructions several times, and made a note of all the stuff I'd need. I went to the Home Depot, and they not only had everything on my list, but a woman there talked me through the procedure. It stinks," she laughed, and met his eyes briefly, "but it's doable. Oh, and I ran into Alice there—of all places to see my daughter. I invited her out for lunch one day next week."

"You're nowhere *near* old enough to be my mother, Lily."

He knew he'd nailed it when she blushed, and didn't immediately answer. Following his instincts, he reached for her hand, brought it to his lips.

As he hoped, her eyes followed the action. When he saw that she focused on him he asked, quietly, "Does it really matter what other people think? How many years are there between your ex and his new wife?"

"That's different."

"That's bullshit, honey. It's okay for a man to be more than twenty years older than his woman, but not okay for a woman to be a dozen or so years older than her lover? Pure bullshit."

"They have a name for women my age who prey on younger men."

"Lucky?"

Lily burst out laughing and Ryan felt his heart lift. If she could laugh, then things weren't that bad.

"No, you nut. They're called *Cougars*."

"Sexy. I like it. But I haven't been your prey yet. Mmm, the very thought of it is getting me hot, though."

"Ryan, I am trying to have a serious discussion here."

"Lily, you're going to have to pick another topic, then. There is nothing wrong with my being fourteen years younger than you are."

"When I'm fifty, you'll only be thirty-six."

"And when I'm eighty, you'll be ninety-four" That one made her snicker. He kissed her palm and placed it on his face. "Sweetheart, we're both adults, and both unattached. That is all that matters. And what we do together is nobody's business but ours. Period."

"Well, tell that to my mother."

"Is it that important to you, that you please your mother?"

"I've tried all my life to please her."

"And never quite succeeded, have you?"

Chapter 11

"No."

He couldn't do anything about the years that separated them, or past hurts. But this issue he could do something about, now.

"Sweetheart, your inability to please your mother has *nothing* to do with you, and everything to do with her. Some people, no matter what, are never happy. Some people refuse to see the positive and focus, instead, on the negative. It's just the way they are."

"I used to think that she hated me, but then I convinced myself *that* couldn't be right. How could a mother hate her own child?"

Ryan knew some mothers did hate their own children. He didn't want to say that, though. He wanted to do whatever he could to ease her heart, help her feel better. Her mother might very well hate her, but there could also be another explanation for her behavior.

In response to Lily's misery, he got up and walked around the table, sat beside her. Sliding his arms around her shoulders, he hugged her close.

"Maybe she doesn't know how to show her love. Not everyone is as open and giving as you are, honey. Some people are trapped by their own emotions, and unable to show what they really feel." He sighed when she relaxed in his arms, and rested her head on his shoulder.

"I have the feeling you're being overly generous where my mother is concerned. And because of that, I'm going to work hard at not letting the years between us bother me."

"It doesn't matter what anyone else thinks, Lily. It only matters what we think. And I *think* we're compatible in enough ways that a few years doesn't make one damn bit of difference."

"We do seem to be getting along even when we're not screwing each other's brains out."

He heard just enough of a 'considering' tone in Lily's voice to make him chuckle. Of all the things he admired about Lily—and there were plenty—her refusal to surrender to negativity ranked right up at the top of the list.

"While you work some more on that desk, why don't I start dinner?"

"You cook?"

"I'm an excellent cook."

Ryan helped Lily up from the table and gave her a hug. Before he let her go, the sound of a car slowing on the road snagged his attention.

Turning, he watched with her as a sleek silver Pontiac pulled into the lane. But rather than coming up toward the house, the vehicle stopped. The driver's door opened and a woman emerged. She waved exuberantly to them, then made her way around to the open trunk of her car.

Ryan tilted his head to the side as the woman went about her business. "What," he said at last, "is that all about?"

He could feel the woman in his arms begin to vibrate.

"Damn it all to hell. That bitch is putting up a 'for sale' sign!"

* * * *

"Hold it right there!"

Lily knew her voice sounded shrill, but she didn't care. She walked as quickly as she could down her laneway, watching with growing dismay as the blonde kept on with her mission, undeterred.

"I said hold it!"

The woman used a heavy mallet to pound the 'for sale' sign into the ground. She looked up as Lily approached, her smile wide.

"I am so, so sorry that I didn't get out this morning, as I promised I would! The meeting with my other clients just dragged on and on. Now, don't you worry about a thing, I've got the papers in my attaché case, and signing them is a mere formality. Since you're so anxious to sell, I've already listed this property on our web site. We don't usually do that before actually getting a signature, but, well, your mother knows my boss, and what can I say? Connections make things happen."

Lily stood speechless for only a moment. Then she blew the hair out of her face, and crossed her arms.

"This property is not for sale."

"Well, of course it is. My boss—"

Lily felt Ryan's hand on her shoulder as he finally caught up to her. "What's the scoop?" he asked.

"Apparently, my mother and…" she frowned, and focused on the blonde. "I'm sorry, what is your name?"

"It's Michelle. Michelle Parsons. Here's my card. Now, if we can just—"

Lily turned her back on Michelle, addressing Ryan. "My mother and Michelle's boss are friends. My guess is that Mother called her friend…" she let the sentence hang. What on Earth could her mother hope to accomplish with this stunt? Did she think Lily so weak willed that the mere *appearance* of a real estate agent with orders from her mother would cow her into selling her home?

Before she could say anything, Ryan shook his head. "Darling, I *told* you the doctor never should have taken your mother off those medications. Though, at least this time, she's only tried to sell your home, and not the CN Tower. But you know what this means. I'm afraid we're going to have to institutionalize her."

Lily chocked back a laugh as a look of horror crossed Michelle's face. Quietly, firmly, she said to the agent, "My home is not for sale. My mother had no right whatsoever to imply otherwise. And, if you don't have my property taken off your company's web site within the next hour, you'll be hearing from my lawyer."

"There must be some misunderstanding. My boss assured me that this property was for sale and…"

While Michelle rambled on, Lily watched as Ryan pulled the sign out of the ground and tossed it back into the trunk of Michelle's car. The real estate agent didn't seem to notice his actions until he relieved her of the mallet, placing it with the sign, and slammed the trunk.

"I am the sole owner of this property and I have no intention of selling." It was all Lily could do to keep her voice calm.

"We'll fax a copy of the deed to your office within the hour just to verify that," Ryan added.

Lily stepped back and indicated Michelle should get back into her car.

"What do I tell my boss?" the woman asked plaintively as Ryan closed the door for her.

"Tell your boss," Lily said sweetly, "to pick better friends."

"What was that supposed to accomplish?" Ryan asked as they watched the Pontiac drive from sight.

"I have absolutely no idea. Usually, my mother is all threats and verbal abuse. This is the first time she's actually *done* anything." She shot Ryan a grin and shrugged. "Maybe she does need medication."

In response, he laughed, then hugged her tight.

"Where do we have to go to fax the deed?"

"You have a copy of it, don't you?"

"Yes, and of the will."

"So you obviously weren't paying attention when we bought your printer. It's a scanner, a copier, a printer, and a fax."

"Well, aren't I just a font of modern technology?"

"Yes, aren't you just?"

* * * *

Lily was pleased that even though he seemed hesitant, Ryan agreed to meet Alice. She couldn't say why she felt on the edge of a new understanding with her daughter, but she did. That insight grew the next week when Alice came to lunch.

"It's been years since I've been out here."

"I know. You protested mightily that summer we spent here with Uncle Mark."

"I remember. I thought the world would come to an end if I couldn't play with my friends. I used to be such a bratty kid."

When Lily could only look at her in astonishment, Alice smiled and shrugged. "Okay, and that flaw is only just abating."

When Alice asked after her furniture-refinishing project, Lily showed her the desk in the barn that needed one more coat of varnish to be done.

"Looks good."

"Thanks."

Walking back toward the house, she paused by the pool. "I remember this as being the only good thing about this place. I'm surprised it's still here and working, though."

"Ryan says Uncle Mark had it completely renovated two years ago. Even then he planned to leave the place to me, and wanted the pool to be in good shape."

"Who's Ryan?"

At just that moment, the roar of a motorcycle broke the afternoon quiet. Lily turned her head and watched appreciatively as Ryan came down the driveway. She saw Alice stare, and couldn't prevent the smile.

"That's Ryan. And before you ask...he's mine."

"Way to go, Mom."

Lily felt a sense of giddiness as those words washed over her. Upon joining them, Ryan kissed her quickly before turning his attention to Alice. Lily found that only a little embarrassing.

Lily further relaxed as Ryan and Alice seemed to hit it off, thick into a discussion of music and movies by the time lunch was being served.

After eating, Ryan took his leave, explaining he had some catch-up work to do for his latest client. Alone over tea, Lily wondered what Alice thought as she studied her mother. So she asked.

"You've changed."

"How so?"

"You didn't apologize once."

"I had nothing to apologize for."

"That never stopped you in the past."

Lily grinned when her daughter lowered her head and said, "Sorry, that wasn't nice."

"Now who's apologizing? You're right, honey. But I thought I did. Maybe I'm finally growing up."

"No, maybe you finally have someone in your life who treats you with respect. And I'm sorry that, in the past, I haven't."

"I didn't give you a whole lot to respect. I let your grandmother, your father, and even your brother, to some extent, bully me. I couldn't see it then. I do now. I'm trying to change, but it's…hard."

"We should have lunch more often," Alice said.

Lily beamed back at her. "We should. But not tomorrow."

"Oh…what happens tomorrow?"

"My first ride on Ryan's motorcycle."

* * * *

"Sweetheart?"

"Yes?"

"You don't have to hold me quite so…securely."

"But I might fall off."

"You won't fall off."

"Okay."

Ryan couldn't help but chuckle when Lily screamed and clutched him even tighter as he fed the motorcycle some gas. True to his word, he kept the speed down, barely going twenty miles per hour as he navigated the bike around the outside edge of the cornfield. Lily hung on to him as if her very life depended on it.

"I'm going to take it into a slow turn. Feel the way the bike moves, Lily. You have to learn to ease up enough so that you can lean into the turn with me."

"No. I'll slide off it."

"You won't slide off it. I promise."

The first turn challenged Ryan's skills to keep the bike from falling—he'd rarely had anyone on the back, and rarely taken a turn so slowly. But despite Lily's litany of "Oh no, oh no, oh no, oh no," they made it around the first corner, approaching the second. By the third time around the field, Ryan could tell by the way Lily had eased her grip that she felt more at secure.

"Okay back there?"

"So far so good."

"Want to try once around the block?"

"You mean…on the road?"

"Yeah. It's the middle of the day, and there's not much traffic. I'll keep well under the speed limit." He felt her head resting on his back for a moment.

"All right. Just once. That'll be like…ten miles in all, won't it?"

"About that. Ready?"

"Ready."

Riding his motorcycle had become one of Ryan's purest pleasures. He hadn't realized, until this very moment, how much he wanted Lily to find pleasure in it, too.

"Turning left up here," Ryan said. The turns around the cornfield had all been right turns. He smiled when he felt Lily lean into the turn with him.

"You doing all right back there, Lily?"

"Doing okay here. The road is smoother than the field."

Ryan smiled. When Lily had insisted riding around the property first, he'd known the ride would be rough—which in turn made the road seem smoother, and thus less dangerous—in comparison. That had been his plan.

"What do you think, sweetheart? The view is different than in a car, isn't it?"

"I'll let you know as soon as I open my eyes."

Ryan roared with laughter, and gunned the accelerator, shooting the bike ahead just a few yards before he pulled it back down to the promised speed. Lily's scream had died off by the time he'd slowed it back down.

"It is a different view. You don't have the same sense of speed in a car as you do here."

"What is it that you're really feeling, sweetheart?"

"Free."

* * * *

Lily liked the way the desk turned out, but couldn't prevent her critical eye from examining it closely even as Ryan looked it over.

"You did a fantastic job. Did you enjoy it?"

"Yeah. Hard work, but as I kept at it and the old varnish and marks faded, and the bare wood emerged, I felt as if I was creating it. You know?"

"You have a real sense of accomplishment in it."

"I do. Housework and laundry—those have always been the never-ending story. But this will last. And when I feel as if I can't do anything, I can look at this desk and know that I can."

"Sweetheart, I believe you can do anything you put your mind to."

Lily couldn't describe the sense of wonder and joy that filled her. No one, absolutely no one had ever given her a compliment that meant as much. She turned, wrapped her arms around Ryan, and kissed him.

It was like sinking into safety and seduction all at the same time. His tongue eagerly responded to hers, his arms quick to wrap around her and his hands to explore. Every time she moved into him like this, she half expected the magic between them to have vanished. But of course it never did, it just kept growing stronger

"Do you trust me, Lily?"

The question vibrated wetly along her neck where Ryan's lip and tongue ignited the flames within her. His hands had moved from her ass to her shoulders, then along each arm until their fingers linked. Gently, he drew her arms behind her back.

"Of course I do."

"Good. Your safe word is 'desk.'"

"Safe word?"

"When you want me to stop, all you have to do is say your safe word."

Before his meaning could fully register, Lily felt the snap of cold steel around her wrists.

Chapter 12

"Now, don't struggle. The steel might bruise your wrists."

"Ryan?" The sound of his name shivered off her lips. She felt a deep flutter in the pit of her belly, and knew that lick of arousal would spread.

"You have only two duties, Lily. Obey and submit."

He turned her around so that he stood behind her. She felt his grip, a hand on each arm, and walked in the direction he guided her.

Once, many years ago, this barn housed horses. The stalls that had been fashioned decades before Lily had been born still remained. All had long since been cleaned out, kept totally empty.

All except one.

The stall at the very back in the northwest corner had been redecorated. A chain with a lock hung from the ceiling. More chains rested on the slats that formed the sides of the enclosure. A blanket covered a part of the floor, and along the wall, on a series of nails, hung some of the toys Lily had seen in the adult novelty store.

"What—"

"Obey and submit. Your first order is: Do not speak unless I give you permission."

Lily swallowed hard and gave a jerky nod in response. She felt both nervous and excited. But she wasn't afraid. She knew Ryan would stop if she asked him to.

"I thought perhaps I might invest in a set of wooden stocks. I think I like the image of you, naked, restrained in that way. I might install it outside the back door of the barn. We'll see how we like this, first."

Lily held still when he ordered her to, wondering just what he intended to do with all those chains. Two of the slats that helped form the rectangle of the stall had been removed, so that the ones that remained measured waist height and lower.

In the next few moments, Lily learned the purpose of the chains.

"Are you in any discomfort, Lily?"

He arranged her so she bent at the waist, with her hands still bound behind her back. He'd ordered her to spread her legs, and chained them to the rails. She now wore a collar around her neck and one of the chains—the lightest one—connected her collar to the chain that hung from the roof while yet another ran to the lowest slat. She couldn't straighten up, could only hold this bent-at-the-waist position, and couldn't close her legs. Ryan had placed a thick, soft pad between her belly and the wood. She could relax, taking the strain off her own muscles. She felt moisture gather between her legs and tried to flex her pussy to enjoy the heat swirling within her.

"No."

"I think under the circumstances, that should be, 'No, master.'"

Licking dry lips, Lily said, "No, master."

"Good girl. Now, let's just adjust your clothing."

He slid his hands around her waist and moved them up, cupping and squeezing her breasts. She felt cool air assail her flesh as he lifted her tee shirt. He worked it completely up to her neck and over her head, exposing her bra. When he released the bra's closure and the undergarment hung, her nipples tightened in anticipation. Technically, her shirt and bra remained on her body. But her breasts hung bare and her nipples hardened even more when he pinched them. The kiss of pain arrowed straight to her pussy, and she couldn't help the whimper.

"Now for the shorts."

He didn't pull them down very far—Lily realized they wouldn't go down very far with the way her legs were spread. But he uncovered her ass. The now useless shorts he'd pushed down had bunched together at the top of her thighs.

"I'll replace the panties."

Lily recognized the snipping sound. Her eyes widened and her heart raced as she realized he'd cut the silky undergarment from her body. She couldn't help the groan as Ryan's hand caressed her naked bottom, as it dipped between her ass cheeks and petted her bare pussy. She felt her hips arching, seeking more of his touch as he played his fingers briefly inside her.

"You're wet already. Do you have any idea how arousing that is for me, to find this kind of a welcome waiting?"

"No. Master."

The deep chuckle sent more shivers coursing through her. She heard him moving behind her but had no idea what he did. The suspense added to her arousal.

"Look what I have for you. Do you know what it is?"

Lily focused on the object Ryan held in front of her face.

"It's…it's a paddle, master."

"No, it's *your* paddle, Lily. And I'm going to use it on you. Right now."

He put one hand between her legs, stroking back and forth over her clit as he landed the first blow with the paddle. The loud smack of leather-covered wood connecting with bare flesh rang through the silent afternoon. It didn't sting very much, and the little sound she made came more because of the suddenness of the act than any sense of pain.

"Again."

This time, he swatted her a bit harder, and Lily's yelp was a reaction to the bite of the paddle on her flesh. Ryan's fingers entered her pussy and her moan and the roll of her hips, totally involuntary, gave Ryan all the permission he needed to continue.

"Lord, honey, this is turning me on."

Lily would have agreed, but Ryan began a steady rhythm of smacks that soon had her gasping for air. The sting flirted on the edge of real pain, and Lily couldn't believe she wanted *more*. The faster Ryan landed the paddle on her naked ass, the higher her arousal climbed. She didn't speak, but when the strangled sound of need escaped her throat, he must have agreed.

The paddle hit the floor only a moment before his pants. She heard the sound of the condom going on, and then she felt his hot, hard cock slamming into her from behind.

* * * *

Ryan buried his cock to the hilt.

The hot tight clasp of Lily's pussy had to be the most wonderful feeling in the world. He began to thrust fast and deep, Lily's hips held firmly between his hands, but not firmly enough to prevent her counter-thrusts. From her gasps and groans, he knew her orgasm neared. The sensation of the squeeze of her inner muscles, and the heat from her pinked bottom against his lower belly made it nearly impossible for Ryan to hold back his own orgasm. Reaching both arms around her, he pinched a nipple with his left hand and found her clit with his right.

Lily cried out as she came, and Ryan's cock, thrusting in her hot release, erupted in its own fountain of pleasure.

For long moments afterward, all their energy went to breathing. Neither could speak. Ryan rested his head on Lily's back, his legs trembling with the effort to keep himself on his feet.

"You all right, sweetheart? I wasn't too rough?"

"I'm terrific."

"You sure as hell are."

Lily giggled, then said, "No, you weren't too rough. In fact, for a moment there, I wanted you to…"

"Honey, if I hit you any harder, it would leave a mark."

"Hmm," she responded.

It only took him a few moments to release her from her bonds, and when he did, before he helped her fix her clothes, he gathered her into a hug. He treated them both to a long slow and luscious kiss, his tongue sampling every bit of her mouth.

Once inside the house again, they showered together, then stretched out on Lily's bed. Ryan cradled her in his arms, playing his hand up and down her back.

"That turned me on more than I thought it would," she said softly.

"Me, too."

It had, in fact, frightened him just a little. Not for anything would he hurt Lily, and the idea—now that his cock lay flaccid between his legs—of putting any marks on her repelled him. But while out in that barn, while she had been restrained and helpless and begging for more, he'd been tempted.

Seeing this new side of himself made him more than a little uncomfortable.

* * * *

Lily worked at the kitchen table, the tools she would need lined up like soldiers waiting to enter battle.

Having gone through her uncle's aging family photo albums, she'd spotted her newly re-finished secretary desk in two pictures, taken when her uncle and mother had both been young. The desk sat in the kitchen in those days, and appeared to be where her grandfather did all his bill paying and her grandmother wrote letters. It had a darker finish then than the one Lily had just given it. But the glass in the doors of the top part had been etched, and *that* detail, she had been able to duplicate.

She'd been torn between wanting the professionals at the glass center to install the two thin panes, and wanting to do it herself. In the end, she chose to see to this final detail personally. If she did end up breaking the glass, well, it would be a simple matter to order two new panes and allow the pros to do it.

The sharp double-pointed fasteners she used to keep the panes in the doors proved difficult to secure; she had to tap them with the tiny hammer hard enough that they would penetrate the wood but not hard enough to break the glass. As she worked, she became aware of the sound of rain falling.

Ryan had gone to the city a few hours before. It had been sunny when he left. She hoped he'd made it home before the rain had started.

She finished tapping in the last fastener when the sound of thunder, and the sound of a revved up Harley-Davidson pierced the quiet.

Setting her tiny hammer down, Lily moved to put the kettle on. A nice cup of tea would do wonders to warm a rain-wet man. And if that didn't work, Lily thought with a smile, she knew something else that would.

Looking out the window, she watched for him. Just when she began to wonder if something was wrong, he emerged from the building. She knew her mouth formed a perfect 'O' in shock. Carrying his leathers, and his helmet, and he was covered in mud.

"Ryan! What happened?"

"Damn tri-axel passed me on the eighth concession. There's one mother of a pothole there, he timed it just perfect to splash me, and I avoided becoming road kill by putting the Hog into a field."

"You're not hurt?" She ran anxious hands over him, only somewhat relieved when he swooped in for a fast kiss.

"I'm fine, sweetheart—but muddy. That's just the kind of field I landed in. I had my jacket off, hoping to spare it as I hauled the bike out of the muck. And yes, the bike is fine, too. I just need to wash it. But first, I need to wash myself."

Lily offered to relieve Ryan of his outer clothes, but he wouldn't hear of her 'cleaning up his mess,' as he put it. He told her she'd done enough, throwing some of his clothes in with hers from the day before, so that he had clean and dry clothes waiting for him upstairs. Turning the burner under the kettle down, she left him to deal with his muck, promising tea and cookies when he came downstairs again.

Taking first one and then the other of the bookcase doors into the living room, Lily began the last step of hanging them back on the desk.

It was tricky to hold onto the door while at the same time setting the screws in the hinges. But after only a few tries, she succeeded.

Standing back to admire her accomplishment, movement outside caught her attention.

Two cars turned into her driveway. The first, a dark blue, two-door sedan, appeared to be driven by a woman. But the second car had all of her attention—white, with a blue stripe down the side and a light bar across the top. Lily had precious little time to wonder why the police were paying her a visit.

Chapter 13

The woman had short red hair, wore a dun-brown suit, and looked as if she sucked lemons for a living. The cop was tall, grim-faced, and trailed behind the woman. Lily didn't wait for them to knock. Opening the door, she knew the expression she wore conveyed her confusion.

"May I help you?"

"Are you Lily Catharine Martin?"

The cop asked that, his voice sounding as unpleasant as he looked. Lily blinked. It had been many years since anyone had used her full name.

"Yes." Then it hit. The awful dread every parent knows is lurking just out of sight. Her heart pounding in her chest, she opened the door wide. "Is it one of my kids? Are they all right? Has there been an accident?"

"No, ma'am. We need to come in, Mrs. Martin. We have a very serious matter to discuss with you."

"Well…all right." Lily's heart still pounded hard in her chest. But that didn't stop her from taking in the way the cop stood, or the hard look on his face. She didn't like the way he had his hand resting on his gun—as if he expected to have to use it.

"Would you like to sit—"

"I'm Ms. Hardy from Children's Aid. This is Constable Ross. We're here to investigate a complaint we've received about you."

Completely confused, Lily could only shake her head. Not only had the words Ms. Hardy said made no sense at all, when Lily automatically offered her hand in greeting, the woman drew back as if Lily carried some communicable disease.

"A complaint? *About me*? To Children's Aid?"

"You have someone living here, a minor male."

"No, I don't. I live here alone."

"Staying with you, then."

"There are no children here. I moved in barely two months ago, and there has never been a child, of any gender, here."

"Indeed. According to our source, you have one Ryan Kincaid, a minor child, if not living here, then staying with you."

"Who the hell told you that? Ryan doesn't live here and he certainly is not a minor—"

"We are not at liberty to reveal our source, but we consider this source to be unimpeachable. Would you please tell us where he is?"

"Ryan?"

"Yes, Ryan Kincaid. Where is he?"

"That can't be any of your business. Ryan is not a—"

At just that moment, the shower in the upstairs bathroom came on.

"No children here, and no one lives here with you?" The social worker shot her a look of contempt. "Did you really expect to deceive us? We'll just see."

Clearly, Ms. Hardy didn't believe her, and she intended to go upstairs to see for herself.

Lily moved to block the intrusive woman. But before she budged even a foot, Constable Ross grabbed her arm and held her fast. He nodded to Mrs. Hardy, then forced Lily into a chair. "You just sit there, Mrs. Martin. And place your hands flat on the table where I can see them."

Though angry and confused, Lily wasn't stupid. She obeyed the officer. Keeping her eyes focused on him, she followed the sound of the other woman's footsteps. She knew when the woman reached the top of the stairs, and when she entered the bedroom. Lily cringed as she imagined the shock that Ryan would receive any moment now.

She shook her head slowly, trying to understand. This played like a scene out of a bad movie. *Where in the name of all that's holy did these people get the idea that Ryan was a minor?* A whisper echoed across her mind and she recalled her mother's accusation the other day. Just then, she heard the bathroom door open. A female scream followed by a male yell made Constable Ross jump. In response to the feminine sound of distress, he began to fumble for his gun.

Lily had had enough. "Oh, for crying out loud, don't be an asshole. Ms. Hardy screamed because she walked in on a grown man's shower and saw his dick."

"Who the fuck are you? Shit lady, I'm showering here!" Ryan's outraged shout drowned out whatever the nosy social worker said. Lily tuned them both out, as she tried to comprehend how her mother could have possibly *believed* she would harm a child—in any way. Numbness descended on her. She'd known, she'd always known deep down inside her mother didn't like her. But she'd believed, all these years, that her mother had at least come to respect her as a wife, and a mother. She'd never done a single thing in her entire life that would lead her mother to think her capable of such a heinous act as she'd reported to the authorities.

Some people, no matter what, are never happy. Some people refuse to see the positive and focus instead on the negative. It's just the way they are.

Ryan's words came back to Lily, and for the first time, she began to consider a new concept. Her mother's behavior all these years really had nothing to do with Lily at all.

Lily's head snapped up when a blushing, rushing Ms. Hardy ran back into the kitchen. Why she ran became clear when a very angry and wet Ryan stormed into the room after her. Covered by only a towel, furious as the gods, he was an impressive sight.

"Who the hell do you think you are barging in on a man that way? And who the hell *are* you, anyway?"

Lily smiled. "Ms. Hardy, Children's Aid, please meet Ryan Kincaid. As you can see, there is absolutely nothing minor about him."

Lily couldn't say who, of the three people in her kitchen with her, appeared the most shocked.

"You're Ryan Kincaid?" The cop's voice dripped with disbelief

Lily could see Ryan putting two and two together very quickly.

"Wait here," he ordered as he turned and raced back upstairs. No one in the kitchen moved, or said a word. Lily didn't know if she wanted to laugh or cry. A burning sensation began in her stomach, and for a moment, she thought that she might be sick. But the moment passed, and in the place of nausea a fine, shimmering anger grew.

Ryan returned in less than three minutes. He'd pulled on his clean jeans. In his hand, he held his wallet. Opening it, he tossed three things onto the table: his driver's license, his health card, and a credit card.

"If you need to see my passport, I'll have to go next door, to my house, and get it."

Constable Ross picked up Ryan's driver's license, examining it closely. "If you live next door, why are you showering here?"

"None of your fucking business."

Lily slowly got to her feet. "Obviously, your unimpeachable source is quite impeachable. I would suggest, very strongly, that you both leave here. Now."

When Ms. Hardy looked as if she would argue further, the Constable simply shook his head. "This has been a mistake. There's no crime here. I'm sorry for the inconvenience."

The intruders left, leaving Lily alone with Ryan. She could tell he was still pissed by his breathing.

"I...I don't know what to say. How to apologize to you for—"

"Don't you dare apologize for what just happened here."

"I think I really do have to apologize. There's only one person who could have been responsible for this. Remember my mother's phone call, and her nasty accusation? But...but I thought she only said that to get under my skin. I never thought she actually believed..." Lily sat down because she had begun to shake. She was so grateful when Ryan sat next to her and put his arms around her.

"That cop didn't get rough with you, did he?"

She heard the concern in his voice, and didn't think, all things considered, that she deserved it. "A little pushy, but nothing, really."

"You promised me tea and cookies."

Lily looked up then and her gaze locked with Ryan's. She couldn't hold back the tears, and when he gathered her more tightly into his arms, she clung to him. And cried silent tears of misery onto his chest.

* * * *

"I don't know what to do," Lily said quietly.

Ryan helped himself to another sugar cookie, breaking it in half, dipping one piece into his tea. Popping the sodden cookie into his mouth, he considered the situation. He didn't know what to do, either. But his concern wasn't so much what to do about Lily's mother, as the woman herself. He could see her sliding into a pit of guilt and shame. He needed a rope to yank her out.

"Well, we ignored the real estate episode, thinking that she might call and you could act as if nothing at all had happened. A harmless stunt, that."

"And this wasn't so harmless."

"I don't think I have a word strong enough in my vocabulary for what she just did to you."

"Me? You're the one violated. So to speak."

"Big deal. Some sexually repressed broad saw my cock. Your own mother, on the other hand, set you up. What if I hadn't been here? What if that cop had arrested you?" Just the thought of it had Ryan's stomach churning. He'd been arrested once, in his younger days. It had been a mistake, but before that mistake had been ironed out, he'd been stripped and searched. The cops hadn't been overly nice about it, either. Thinking of Lily being put through that infuriated him.

"The important thing is you *were* here, and I wasn't arrested."

But she had been humiliated. Ryan could still see the remnants of it on her face. He knew it would be a long, long time before memories of today would come easy.

"What do you want to do?"

"Well, there's what I want to do and what I can do. I want to go right over to my mother's house and smack her across the face. And that shames me."

"You'd never do that, really. But to want to? Who wouldn't? Don't let the urge shame you, sweetheart. It's a natural enough one." One, in fact, Ryan had entertained briefly, himself.

"In the past, she would interfere, harass, and insult, until everyone close to me agreed with her. But she's never done anything like this before. Did she think, somehow, that causing trouble for me would push you away?"

"If that's her plan, she's doomed to failure."

He waited until Lily looked him in the eye. "Nothing, and no one, could ever make me turn away from you, sweetheart."

He saw it in her eyes, the emotion, and the response that he had been hoping for. All things considered, he didn't mind being the one to say it first. And it would be a first. He'd never said these words to a woman before.

Swallowing his pride, he picked up her hand and kissed it. "I love you, Lily. I love you almost beyond reason."

He watched as tears filled her eyes. The smile that began to spread across her face warmed him to his very soul.

"I love you, too. I thought to just have an affair with you. But I love you so much. Will you hold on to me? I need to feel your arms around me. I need to feel safe there, knowing you love me."

"Come here, sweetheart."

This need went beyond sex. Ryan scooped her onto his lap and enfolded her within his arms. He needed this, too. This closeness of heart, soul and spirit. This unity of two into one. Together, they forged a fortress against the rest of the world that could sometimes be cruel and unfair.

"We love each other, Lily. As long as you hang onto that, then no one and nothing can touch us."

Chapter 14

For Lily, nothing could overshadow the glorious bloom of being in love. What Ryan had said—that some people refused to see the positive—kept playing over and over in her mind. By the next day, she realized she'd turned a corner when at last she understood. In the past, whenever her mother expressed disappointment, accusing her of whatever flaw struck her fancy, Lily would allow the hurt and the guilt to eat away at her, and to cow her. But now, she could look back over her life with new eyes, seeing through the layers of quilt and acquiescence.

Lily never had been the cause of her mother's coldness. Finally gratefully, she let go of the past.

She felt remade, and free. Though late summer, it could have been spring for the emotions coursing through her. Her life stretched ahead of her with endless possibilities.

Ryan had returned to his own place for a few hours. He needed to work, and while she enjoyed every minute spent with him and knew he felt the same, they each appreciated time alone. Lily used hers to take care of the household chores. As she did her housework this day, she performed more than just routine cleaning. As she worked, she envisioned the possibilities. Oh, she had ideas of things she could do to this house, painting and decorating and freshening that would make it perfect—that would make it *hers*. Styles she'd always loved but had never been able to embrace, whims she'd had to ignore, whatever she wanted to do, she could do.

Perhaps she always could have done so. Perhaps all she ever would have had to do in the past was to put her foot down, stand up for herself, and refuse to be intimidated, or dominated. But she had never believed in herself before. Lily laughed right out loud, and didn't care. She didn't have to look far to know why she believed in herself now.

Because Ryan truly loved her, truly believed in her, she could love and believe in herself. She had confidence in herself as a person. She felt…God, she felt like a whole woman for the first time in her life!

New horizons didn't have to be about doing, after all. They could just as easily be about being. Each new dawn brought a wonderful new day. Life was, finally and at last, something to be *lived*.

Everything in her home would be renewed and fresh and vital, and she would begin at the top and work her way down. Filled with energy, she gathered cleaning supplies and garbage bags and ran up to the second story, then up the small staircase to the attic. So what if she decided to do spring cleaning in August? She could do any damn thing she pleased.

"Oh, my."

She'd avoided the attic before today, and now she wondered if she hadn't suspected that here awaited a job with a capital 'J'.

Boxes had been stacked on top of boxes, taking up nearly every bit of floor space—of which there was not a great deal to begin with.

She inhaled deeply and closed her eyes. Scent, she knew, formed the strongest and oldest memory. She could recall coming up here with her grandfather when she'd been little more than a child. It smelled exactly the same now, as then. This scent Lily would forever associate with that man she could barely otherwise remember. Perhaps, she thought, this was the scent of history, of roots. Opening her eyes, she surveyed the cramped space. Two old steamer trunks had been tucked under the eaves, and Lily wondered if she would find treasures within, or only trash. Some of the cartons looked brand new, and she thought Uncle Mark had done a bit of cleaning and organizing of his own before he died.

Sitting on the landing, she pulled one of the newer boxes closer, and opened it. She would make three piles, she decided. What she would keep, what she would donate to some charity, and what could be thrown away.

This first box contained papers, mostly correspondence addressed to her grandmother. Since the letters had been sent *to* Millicent Robertson, she thought most of them might be trash. But she found a few items concerning the Women's Institute, the Garden Club, and the Ladies' Auxiliary at the church that the local heritage society might want. A stack of letters tied together with a ribbon caught her eye. A quick flip through showed them all addressed to her grandmother from someone named Corrine Westerly of Toronto. At the bottom of the box, a leather-bound book waited. Curious, Lily pulled it out. No title or etching graced the outside of it. But she had only to open the cover to know what she held.

Dated January 1950, this diary had belonged to Eloise Robertson—Lily's mother.

* * * *

All the time that Ryan worked to finish up his current software program, anger grew within him. He couldn't seem to let it go.

He'd been eleven when his own mother had died, the result of a car accident. He remembered homemade soup on cold winter days and fresh chocolate chip cookies after school. He remembered that even when there wasn't much money about, his mother managed to make a fine Christmas. He remembered being cuddled in the wake of nightmares, and having his forehead bathed through the night when he'd been very sick with measles.

And he realized Lily likely had been given none of those kinds of memories. Ryan had always held that parents, being parents, deserved respect. But now he had to rethink that view. How could anyone respect a mother who would accuse falsely, or out of spite? Had it indeed truly been spite, or did Lily's mother really believe a false impression John had fed her?

Lily had decided to do nothing in response to her mother's actions. And on principal, he agreed with her. If the old bat wanted to stir trouble between the two of them, the best response would be to act as if her interference meant nothing at all.

However, he was having a hell of a hard time letting it go. Someone had attacked the woman he loved, and he needed to *do* something. If the villain had been a man, he'd have already sought the bastard out and punched him in the face. But of course, he couldn't do that to Lily's mother.

It wouldn't hurt, though, to see how much information he could get on the woman. He had a vague notion of where she lived, but no idea what she looked like. He wanted specifics. He excelled at finding answers, and investigating. And while in investigator mode, he'd snoop out the particulars on her ex-husband, too.

If trouble came looking for them again, he wanted to damn well be ready for it.

* * * *

"How did I ever manage to live without a pool before now?"

"My question would be how did you manage to live without swimming naked before? You seem very comfortable in your skin these days, my Lily."

Floating on her back with her eyes closed, she smiled. She was comfortable in her skin, and not just when it came to skinny-dipping. "Mmm, I am. This is the only way to decompress after a heavy day of attic cleaning."

"No, it's not."

"All right, I'll rephrase that. This is the only way to *begin* to decompress."

Lily sensed him coming closer, even with her eyes still closed. When she felt his touch, a hand caressing a breast, it didn't startle her at all. She simply enjoyed.

"So if this is the beginning, what comes next?" The airflow from his huskily whispered question vibrated against her wet nipple. His sucking, as always, aroused her. Reaching out, reaching down, she stroked his already hard cock.

"This time," she replied, "you're going to be the one tied up."

Getting out of the pool, they dried quickly. Then Lily took his hand, leading him inside. She'd chosen the bedroom. She'd been planning this for most of the afternoon. She'd made certain preparations ahead of time, confident that he would let her have her way with him.

He certainly didn't disappoint her.

She used some braided cords she found in the attic. The drapes they'd been attached to she'd trashed, but the cords themselves felt soft, silky, and despite their age, still had incredible strength. Ryan looked good, spread out on her bed, each arm tied to the headboard, each leg leashed to a leg of the bed.

Over his eyes, she tied a black, silken scarf.

"So…what's my safe word?"

Lily raised one eyebrow. "Do you need one?" And she ran a hand down over his chest and continued on to gently to stroke his groin.

"Well…you know…in the interest of fair play."

She bent over him and laid her mouth on his. Her tongue dipped and teased his, then licked the corner of his mouth.

"Very well. Your safe word is 'fair play.'"

Lily had never had a man at her mercy before. She'd never had someone trust her so completely, or hand control over to her so totally. Doing so, he'd given her the most incredible high she'd ever known. Not a feeling of power, so much, as a sense of *empowerment*. Ryan had been the first, the only, who treated her as a person of value. He asked for everything, but was willing to give everything in return.

She could give him all that she held in her heart, and he would cherish the gift.

She opened the bedside table drawer, and withdrew the first item she'd secreted there. Long, lush, and purple, the feather had caught her fancy. She used it now to gently trace, back and forth, from one male nipple to the other.

"Soft," he said, then frowned.

She understood his frown, totally. "Yes, you may speak freely. I've never done this before. I want to know how it feels…what you think…what you want."

She giggled when he squirmed as the feather brushed against his armpits. She licked and nibbled his nipples while she used the feather to caress his cock and scrotum, She purred in pleasure when his hips strained. How alike they behaved in this, their sex seeking the touch of the other even when that seeking was thwarted.

"I've been thinking a long time about this," Lily confessed as she reached into the drawer. "You kept repeating that word 'everything,' and hearing it over and over again opened the door to my imagination." She pulled out one of the toys she'd borrowed from the barn. A piece of leather, about five inches long and two wide, she'd tested it on the inside of her arm that very afternoon.

She let one finger trail from the base of his cock to the knob. How beautifully swollen the head, how rigid the shaft. Truly glorious, half pink, half beige, and all hers. She waited until Ryan groaned in bliss. Then she brought the strap down on his hip.

"Shit." He cursed and jumped at the same time.

"I begin to see the appeal in this. How did that feel?"

"Do it again."

"Some place, a bit more sensitive, maybe." As she continued to stroke his cock, she brought the strap down on the inside of his right thigh.

"Fuck, that's...different."

"Unpleasant?"

"Not entirely."

She knew the truth of his words, for his cock had hardened and strained perceptibly.

"I'll use it again, but you won't know when until it happens."

Getting up from the bed, she walked over to her dresser and picked up her digital camera.

"Your cock is very photogenic."

She smiled when he frowned, as he considered, she imagined, being on the other end of the lens. "Especially when I use the zoom," she added, delighted with his blush. Setting the camera aside, she took another item from a cup on her dresser, then detoured into the bathroom for the bottle of massage oil, that she'd set in a bowl of warm water. Sitting again on the edge of the bed, her left hand enveloped his cock, and began a slow, measured stroking.

"I love the feel of your cock in my hand. It's so hot and hard, yet the skin is silky soft. Mmm, it is so very, very hot and getting hotter. Oh, and Ryan? Don't come."

"Sweetheart, that feels wonderful, so good...holy shit!"

Lily held an ice cube against his shaft, and began to slide it up and down. Her fingers stroked against his flesh and against his belly and aroused him. The ice cube, she held between her palm and the other side of his rod.

"Good?"

"Damn, honey, when you open your imagination, you really open it. Good. Powerful. Too much and not enough at the same time."

"Cold, darling?"

"Fucking freezing."

"Let me just fix that for you."

She tossed the remainder of the ice cube into the bowl of water. Then, liberally, she began to dribble the warmed massage oil on his penis. The scent of strawberries filled the air.

"Don't come and don't piss myself."

"Oops. Didn't think of that. I guess you need me to rub it in, huh?"

Oiled, silky smooth and warm, her hands made love to his cock as she massaged him, a gentle up and down motion. Every other pass, she'd drag her hand down to cup his balls and give them a gentle squeeze. The musky scent of sex mingled with the tart-sweet aroma of the berries, and Lily's mouth watered.

"I really need to come soon, sweetheart," Ryan said through gritted teeth.

"In a minute. You neglected to tell me something about this oil."

"What...mmm, babe...what didn't I tell you?"

"You didn't tell me how it tastes."

With that Lily took his cock into her mouth. He was large, and her lips stretched wide to take him in. Her hand continued to envelop and stroke, and her mouth followed. She took him deep, and had to breathe carefully when the tip of his penis hit the back of her throat and nearly made her choke. Deciding she couldn't keep him that deep, she made up for the deficiency by playing her tongue up and down his shaft and taking up a rhythmic sucking.

"Lily...for the love of...let me *come!*"

She released his cock with a wet *plop*. "You want to come, lover? What's it worth to you?"

Chapter 15

Ryan thought he would explode.

He'd never been so hard, so hot, and so desperate to come. Lily's question bounced around in his head, not making any sense—then making all the sense in the world.

"Everything, Lily. It's worth everything. You're worth everything."

"Come for me, Ryan. Come when you want to."

He closed his eyes, holding on because the feel of her mouth and hand pleasuring his cock went beyond wonderful. That sweet, long moment when arousal reached an impossible height was a place too rarely visited. The soft slick glide of her lips and tongue became the center of his world. He fought hard to stay in this place of erotic bliss. And then she took him deep and began to suck harder and more insistently.

His strangled shout of completion bounced against the walls. It felt as if his sperm exploded right out of him. He came and came with no sense of time or space, just this orgasm, the fiercest he'd ever known. Sliding down on the other side, his body bucked and shivered, as if a thousand volts of raw electricity had zapped him.

Lily's mouth continued to work his cock.

"Ah...sweetheart?" he managed after a few moments.

"Mmm?"

"I, ah, think I just came in your mouth."

He felt her let him go, though her hand kept stroking. "I could hardly miss that. First time for me. Very strong and salty. But not bad."

"Um...so why are you..."

"Oh, baby, I'm not done with you yet. I want you hard again. And then I'm going to fuck your brains out."

"You're going to kill me. There'll be nothing left of me but a dried up, used up, shriveled shell."

"Is that a complaint?"

He heard the smile in her voice and wished his hands free so he could hold her close. Instead, he gave her what she needed. "Hell, no. No complaints here. Just…be gentle with me."

The next instant, he yelped, as the strap had landed smartly against his hip.

"No promises there, sweetheart. But I *will* be thorough."

His heart swelled. The uptight, shy woman she'd been mere weeks before had disappeared. Now, his Lily was in full bloom, a beautiful flower of a woman unafraid to spread her petals and be all she could possibly be.

Despite her obvious devotion to the task at hand, he didn't think he'd be able to rise to her challenge anytime soon, but he did. And he knew that thinking about the woman she'd become and how he felt about her helped to trigger his renewed erection.

This time, arousal was a slow, lazy climb. As he felt the heat grow, Lily responded to his groans by rubbing her bare breasts against his legs. Her nipples pebbled, and he found a fierce pride that she would be turned on by pleasuring him.

"Baby, I need you." Unashamed, he let her know how very much he needed her. When she released his cock and slithered up his body, he wanted his hands free so he could touch her. And when she straddled him, when she impaled herself upon him, he thrust his hips high, touching her deeply, in the only way he could.

* * * *

Lily awoke just as the morning sun speared through the bedroom window. Wrapped in Ryan's arms, she mused, had become the only way to start the day. They had made love again and again after she got rid of his bindings. Sometimes hard and fast, sometimes slow and tender, she'd reveled in his touch. They'd barely spoken, but had communicated volumes.

"Do I buy you a black leather g-string and thigh high boots and begin to call you Mistress?"

Lily laughed, then wiggled around so that she lay on top of Ryan.

"Although I found it very interesting, and arousing, I don't think I have a future as a dominatrix. I really didn't like hitting you."

"It didn't hurt, sweetheart."

"I know." Lily traced a finger over Ryan's lips, enjoying the feel of him, marveling at his sheer beauty—though she knew if she told him she thought him beautiful, he'd blush. Leaning up, she kissed him lightly.

"Reg treated me, in many ways, like a child. Or a servant. So it comes as some surprise to me that I became so totally turned on when you tied me up and paddled me. I really liked it. I 'submitted' to you, but I felt far from dominated. I felt...free. Of course, that's more or less how I feel all the time with you. I love you, Ryan."

"Damn good thing, since I love you, too."

She laid her head on his shoulder, and felt his arms come around her. How amazing that this man did everything right for her. All her life, she'd had an enormous amount of love in her heart, love that she'd given to her husband and children and yes, even to her mother. But there had been something missing in the giving. Now, she knew what. Ryan cherished her gift of love, and treasured it. So when she gave it to him, she felt she gave something of value.

And she knew her heart would stay safe in his hands.

"Do you have any plans for the day?"

She sighed and stretched on top of him, wiggling and spreading her legs so that his cock nestled between the folds of her labia. He responded very nicely by holding her tighter and thrusting his hips just a little.

"Besides that," he said.

"I want to weed my veggie garden before the heat of the day hits. You?"

"I need to touch base with the software manufacturer I've been freelancing for. They have an office in Toronto, and I have a ten a.m. appointment."

Lily opened her eyes and turned her head to see the bedside clock. It wasn't yet seven. Sitting up, she began to rub her dewy lips back and forth against him.

"Why don't I give you something to think about while you're gone?"

"What did you have in mind?"

"I want to take your cock deep inside my pussy. I want to fuck you."

"How about if we fuck each other?"

"Sounds like a plan," Lily said as she raised herself up and slowly took his rigid shaft into her body.

* * * *

Lily loved the feel of earth beneath her fingers. She had a three-pronged cultivator that would have done a pretty good job of uprooting the weeds growing between her tomato plants, but she discovered something intrinsically satisfying about pulling the weeds by hand. Her plants produced abundantly, and she knew she needed to find some recipes for chili sauce and tomato paste. She'd already enjoyed one meal of green beans, with more yet to come. The radishes had all been eaten. She'd only planted a few. The half row of carrots was nearly ready, and peppers had sprouted on her green pepper plants. Next year, she thought, she'd plant seeds instead of the plants she'd started with this year. Maybe she'd buy herself a little greenhouse, one made of wood and plastic, and start the seeds early.

At the distinctive sound, she looked up, shocked to see Reg's car coming down the driveway toward her. Once upon a time, she would have begun fidgeting, anxious that he not catch her doing something he hated. It shamed her to realize that would have been her reaction if he'd come to see her the day before Ryan came into her life.

Now, she kept weeding and waited. On the heels of her mother's incursions, she couldn't help but wonder what her ex could possibly want.

She pretended to ignore him as he got out of the car and stood by the closed driver's door. She watched him put his hands on his hips, and understood that he expected her to come to him.

"Tough shit," she mumbled too quietly for him to hear. "You want to visit me, you come over here."

She stole a look at her watch. When he finally gave up and approached, nearly five minutes had passed.

"Lily."

"Reginald."

He hated it, she knew, when she called him that.

"Your mind must have been wandering. I've been here for ten minutes."

"My mind wasn't wandering. I thought you'd forgotten yourself, the way you just stood there, trance-like, by the car. And it's only been five minutes."

She kept weeding, but noted the frown on his face. *I just bet you are confused, you son-of-a-bitch. The little woman isn't bowing and scraping the way she used to.*

"Must you keep playing in the dirt? I need to speak to you."

"I'm an amazing woman. I can play in the dirt and listen to you at the same time. However, since the sight of me weeding the garden seems to upset your delicate sensibility, I'll take a break. We can sit at the picnic table."

"You're not going to invite me in?"

"That's right."

Lily used the garden hose to wash her hands, then shook them to air-dry as she walked over and sat at the picnic table. Taking a moment, she studied her ex. He was still an attractive man. True, over the last couple of years, a paunch had begun to form around his middle. His hairline had retreated rather nicely, but Lily had never minded that. He'd been a handsome devil when she first met him. She remembered the thrill that this university sophomore seemed attracted to her, a lowly high school senior. And, too, it turned out that attracting him had pleased her mother.

She'd loved him on her wedding day, and had gone to his bed a virgin. But years of his constant subtle put-downs, years of his cheating with one woman after another, had eroded and finally destroyed that love. Even without loving him, she would have remained married to him if he hadn't asked for a divorce. She wasn't ashamed of that. She'd taken vows, and had been willing to live by them. The very fact that those vows contained the phrase 'For better or worse' meant there could be a 'worse.' She figured she'd been living that.

When Reg had asked for the divorce, she'd been devastated. Now, she felt profoundly grateful.

"I have a serious matter I need to discuss with you. This 'inheritance' that your uncle has left you should have been anticipated and listed prior to the divorce. It should have figured into the division of properties and assets."

Lily tilted her head to one side. Reg wore his lord-to-peasant expression, the one he tended to use on her in the past when he wanted to give her shit for something. And he spoke as if reprimanding one who had knowingly cheated. She knew he expected her to apologize and make it right. He expected her to feel cowed.

The most amazing thing was that she didn't feel anything, at all. No trepidation, no intimidation, and no worry of any kind existed inside her. Neither did she feel mean-spirited or vengeful. How utterly amazing. Whatever power he used to have over her, apparently, had vanished.

"No, I suppose disclosure wasn't very thorough. Else it would have included your firm, your pension fund that you routed through several numbered companies, and your overseas investment account. But hey, them's the breaks."

"I have no idea what—"

"Save it. You did your damnedest to ensure that I got as little as possible. I had no idea Uncle Mark intended to name me as sole beneficiary. Never even crossed my mind. Further, you arranged the divorce settlement in such a way as to prevent me from having second thoughts down the road and coming after more money. That little codicil works both ways. At the time, it didn't bother you to have it that way. You never imagined any circumstance when you'd want to change it. Again, them's the breaks. Bottom line: This farm is mine, and mine alone. And no one—not my son, not my mother, and certainly not you—can make me sell it."

Lily watched as Reg dealt with the shock of having so logical and intelligent an argument tossed in his face. She'd bet that not only had he believed she'd never read the divorce settlement, he'd probably figured she hadn't understood it.

"Don't you care about your children? It's hardly fair that I'm left to pay every part of their educations, and to support them all by myself without any contribution from you."

"Why isn't it fair? You divorced me, not them. You refused to even consider that I should work outside the home, the entire time we *were* married. Seems to me that you therefore *insisted* on footing the bill all by yourself right from the word go. Why is it a problem for you now? Oh, and by the way, how is Mary?"

The look in Reg's eyes gave Lily a clue. She fought a smile as she considered that perhaps Reg had leapt before he really looked with that one. On the two occasions she'd seen the new Mrs. Martin, the woman had been garbed in designer wear and sporting very nice baubles. Maybe Mary wasn't content to accept an 'allowance.'

"My wife is fine, thank you very much."

"And that's the entire point, Reginald. Mary is your wife, and I am not. My business—what I have, what I do—is none of your business. Not anymore."

"I am beginning to see that perhaps your mother is right. There's something…not quite right with you. I see that I'm wasting my time here. Steps may have to be taken."

"About fifty," Lily said sweetly, "to take you back to your car."

Long after Reg had driven off, Lily sat at the picnic table and thought. She felt good about the way she'd just handled her ex. Never in her entire life had she ever felt in control the way she had just then. For the first time, she'd been able to respond in the moment, rather than thinking of what she could have said afterwards.

But though she believed she'd won that skirmish, the rest of the war, was yet to come.

Reginald Martin might be a pompous ass, but he had intelligence and the reputation for being a savvy lawyer. Her advantage lay in the fact she knew that and him, while he had no clue how her mind worked, at all.

The time had come, she decided, to begin acting as smart as she knew herself to be.

Chapter 16

"That lousy son-of-a-bitch!" Ryan exploded after Lily told him about her ex's visit.

"I handled him all right, I thought."

"You handled him like a pro." And she had. Too bad he hadn't been here at the time. He would have liked to have saved Reg the walk to his car. Ryan had worked as a bouncer once. He still remembered the moves.

"I bet he spent the next couple of hours in review of the entire conversation trying to figure out where he went wrong."

Ryan smiled in response not only to her words, but also to the mischievous little smile that kissed the corner of her mouth. Gnawing at him, though, was the sure and certain belief that Lily's ex had been motivated to visit in the first place by his former mother-in-law.

"I've decided not to wait to find out what 'steps' Reg felt might need to be taken, although, from what both he and my mother have said, I can guess."

Something in Lily's expression intrigued him. "You can guess what it is the dynamic duo is planning to do next?"

"Oh, you bet. Let me tell you how their minds are working. One, I am not doing as I am told—as I have always done. Two, I did not lower my eyes and play the meek and dutiful wife—as I have always done. Three—I actually had the nerve to talk back, which I have *never* done. Mother said it and Reg said it. *There's something wrong with me.*"

Ryan felt his left eyebrow rise. "What the hell are they going to do, try and have you committed?" He thought his comment sarcastic. But when he met Lily's eyes, he saw she believed exactly that.

"Either try to have me committed, or declared incompetent. Of course, Reg, as my ex-husband, could not be appointed as my guardian. But my mother could. "

"They don't have a hope in hell of proving you incompetent."

"Well, you know that, and so do I. And they will, too, once they look into the matter. But see, they're still thinking of how I've always been, and I would be willing to wager they'll decide, after discovering that they couldn't force me to do their bidding by legal means, that they could talk me into committing myself."

"I'm getting chills just thinking about anyone doing that to a family member. And what would be the point?"

"For Reg, it's simple—dollars and cents. His new wife probably isn't as frugal as he would like, and he has the kids tuition and living expenses to shoulder. As for my mother—I'm not sure there is a reason."

Ryan's gut turned sour at the idea Lily's mother would consider such a course. *The old bat. Someone aught to have a come-to-Jesus talk with her.*

When he looked up, Lily beamed at him. That she could smile in the midst of her family's hostility toward her amazed him.

"What?"

"Thank you very, very much for insisting I get a computer. As soon as Reg left this morning, I began doing some research. And while gathering information, I made plans."

She looked so damn proud of herself that Ryan had to give her a hug. "Will you share your plans with me?"

"Of course. They likely need a bit of refining, and you can help with that. But I know exactly what I want to do."

* * * *

He left her early the next afternoon with the excuse that he had a business meeting. He didn't think what he intended to do would take so very long.

He thought Lily's plan was inspired. He couldn't wait to the see the expression on her ex's and son's faces when she laid everything out for them. Ryan had every confidence that when it came to dealing with them, Lily would come out on top.

Her mother was another story.

Mark had mentioned a few things over the years about his sister. Eloise Robertson Riggs had been a sour, bitter teenager and had grown into a sour, bitter woman. From what he could gather, she had made it her mission in life to alienate and then brow beat first her husband and then her child.

Perhaps something had happened in her childhood, some major trauma that had broken her heart and turned her mean. Mark hadn't known because he'd been in the army, fighting in Korea at the time.

But shit happened to a lot of people, Ryan thought. That didn't excuse monstrous behavior.

He went home only long enough to don his leathers. At four on a Friday afternoon, the third Friday of the month, he knew where to find his adversary.

He had it on very good authority that Eloise Robertson Riggs played bridge every third Friday at five p.m. at the Bay Country Club.

He wasn't stupid enough to confront the woman without a bevy of witnesses. And if he just happened to embarrass her in the process—why that would simply be a marvelous bonus.

* * * *

Eloise's eye critically examined the dining room. She felt her pique rise as she noted several tables occupied by patrons who weren't dressed properly. It didn't matter if the club executive had voted last year to relax the dress code on all but the most formal of occasions. The Bay Club used to be an exclusive establishment. Perhaps, she thought bitterly, the time had come to rethink her membership.

She'd worked hard all her life to gain the social stature she enjoyed now. Among her accomplishments, she'd been elected as President of the

Arts Council, President of the Harbor Club, and was the current past President of the Children's Charity Fund. Other women—those she considered above her station—sought her out for her sound advice. Lesser women courted her favor, she suspected, just to be seen with her.

It had taken her fifty years to reach the place she believed should have been hers by right. She nodded once, decision made. If the executive of the Bay Country Club did not see reason when she addressed them next week, she would cancel her membership.

Other, more polished and exclusive clubs would be delighted with her patronage, and pleased to call her one of their own.

As always, she arrived last to the small, intimate meeting room her private group used for its once-a-month gathering. This particular card club had twelve members, making three tables for bridge. Card playing came secondary to being seen, and the general exchange of information. One had to keep up, and this had proven a fairly good venue for that purpose.

"There you are, Eloise. Stylishly late, as usual."

The greeting came from Doctor Margaret Sampson-Drake. Her husband had founded a prestigious law firm, and she herself, before she retired, had been Chancellor of the University. Not that Eloise approved of women working outside the home. But if one felt moved to do as much, one should at least aspire to do so at the top.

"And you, Margaret, ever the schoolmarm taking attendance."

She nodded to some, and air kissed the cheeks of others. Taking her seat at the head of the first table, she had her back to the door.

The gasps alerted her, but before she could even turn around in her chair, a heavy something—she recognized it as a helmet of some sort—landed on the table before her. Two large leather gloves landed on top of it. She looked up and into the angry dark eyes of a scowling hoodlum.

"I beg your pardon?"

"You may very well before I'm done with you."

"I don't know you. Remove yourself from this room at once before I have someone call security." And it did peeve her that none of her group seemed to be moving to do just that.

"I'm hurt. Now, how can you say you don't know me, Eloise, when you reported to the police that I was a minor child being molested by your very own daughter?"

"I don't know what—" she felt her face getting red, and then squirmed even more when the hoodlum snagged an empty chair, turned it around, and sat astride it. He continued to speak loud enough for all in the room to hear him.

"See, here's the deal. I'm sorry for whatever happened in your life that turned you into a miserable, mean, sour old bitch. But I can't have you going around making the life of the woman I love difficult anymore. So you have two choices. Back off, leave her alone, and only have pleasant things to say to her when you call. Or, continue on, as you are, in which case you will be hearing from my lawyers. I'm delicate. Having the police accuse me of being a child traumatized me. Expensively."

"I do believe it will be *you* hearing from *my* lawyers, you young...thug."

"Kincaid. Ryan Kincaid. And sister, you have no idea how happy you've just made me."

* * * *

Lily had no idea if Ryan would be back for dinner, or not. When he left, he hadn't said, but she thought he might be. She almost took the time to throw a meal together before she caught herself. She resolved to stop doing things the way she had always done them in the past.

That meant she wasn't going to assume the responsibility for 'taking care' of Ryan the way she had always taken care of her family. He certainly didn't expect her to cater to him. When he returned, they'd discuss meal options together.

Nodding her head firmly, Lily returned to her list of things to do. She'd already spoken to her physician. Placing a check mark beside his name, she moved on to the next item. The next item read, simply 'Plan Event.'

It had been a while since she'd put together a dinner party. Reg had used them extensively when his firm had been just getting started, and Lily had done a wonderful job of not only organizing, but also preparing the multi-course feasts. But then as the firm prospered, he preferred to have catered affairs at trendy Toronto eateries.

Lily felt torn. Going to a restaurant felt tantamount to airing her dirty linen in public. But at the same time, she really didn't want to host the event at home, either. She didn't want the memories of what could very well turn out to be an ugly scene to flourish here.

But this was her home, the place where she felt most in control. If things got really ugly, she could throw the bastards out.

Another decision made, she thought. Now all she had to decide was the date. As she reached for her calendar, the phone rang.

* * * *

Lily looked up from her cup of tea when Ryan came through the door. By the way he stood there for a moment, she understood that he'd read her mood.

"Are we about to have a fight?"

"I think so, yes."

Ryan seemed to take this news in stride, for he nodded to her once, slipped off his jacket, draped it over another chair, and then took the chair opposite her.

"You told me, this very day, that you thought my plan brilliant."

"I did, I do, and it is."

"I see. But you obviously didn't trust me to take care of the situation, did you? You went and confronted my mother, threatening her."

"You're damn right I did. Do you think I'm going to stand by when the one person in all the world who is supposed to be on your side, instead attacks you?"

"You lied to me, then!"

"I never did! She's your mother, Lily. Can you sit there and actually tell me you could tell your mother to kiss off in the same way you can your ex?

Can you stand against her the way you're standing against me, and scream at the top of your lungs?"

Not trusting her voice, Lily grabbed up her empty tea mug and hurled it against the wall.

"Good shot."

Lily was horrified with herself. She'd never thrown anything in anger in her life. She looked at Ryan, unsure what would happen next—not expecting what actually did.

Chapter 17

With a loud bark of laughter, he rounded the table, grabbed her up and into a passionate kiss.

"Let go of me. Are you crazy? We're having a fight here!"

"So? Our having a disagreement doesn't mean we don't love each other anymore. Does it?"

The startled look on Lily's face told Ryan she did, indeed, think that's what it would mean.

"You can be pissed with me and still love me. And I can be pissed with you and still love you."

"But you took over. Do you have any idea...damn it, Ryan, when you went after my mother, you treated me the same way they did!"

"Oh, now, you're going to get *me* pissed with talk like that. Lily—" he paused, took her hand in his and kissed it. Then he sat down, and settled her in his lap.

"I didn't take over. That wasn't my intention. I just couldn't stand by while she kept hurting you. I'm more than willing to stand back while you fight your own battles. But don't ask me to *never* come to the defense of the woman I love."

When she continued to just stare at him, he kissed her lightly again. "There's a difference, darling, in taking over and *taking care*. Maybe the actions appear the same, on the surface. Where they differ is in the intent— and the heart that lies behind them. The woman is your *mother*. Underneath everything, she's your mother."

"She is. And I don't want to hurt her. I don't want to disrespect her. But I may have to, a little. Not to get even, nor even to vindicate myself. But just to get her to *stop*. The really sad thing is, I don't think there's anything I could do or say—that anyone could do or say—that is ever going to change her."

"Then maybe, sweetheart, the best we can hope for is that she'll leave you be once she realizes there is no potential gain of any kind for her to continue to harass you."

"Maybe. So...how did you 'threaten her in a vile and unspeakable manner?'"

* * * *

John felt good. The phone call from his mother, and the invitation to dinner, could only mean one thing. She had caved. He wasn't surprised. He knew his grandmother had been active, and that his father had gotten involved. He felt so happy, he jumped up and tried to slap the ceiling. Everything he had ever wanted would soon be his.

When he'd opted for a degree in social work, it had been because he thought it would be the easiest degree to get. He'd never dreamed that studying how to 'help' people could so easily be converted to how to help himself. Of course, he'd always been able to get his way. Whether with family or friends, he had only to plant a few ideas, affect a hurt or devastated demeanor, and bam! He got what he wanted.

He pushed aside the sense of dejection that threatened when he thought of how Sheila had dumped him. Old news. Soon he would be so irresistible that he'd have a parade of willing woman through his bedroom.

Focusing on the money he would soon rake in chased away any invading sadness. He thought he'd head out to the Jaguar dealership, pick up the latest brochures. A slow smile spread across his face.

Yes, a Jaguar would absolutely suit the image he wanted to build for himself. With a Jag and an apartment—no, a loft, he decided then and there, on Wellington, near the St. Lawrence market—his life would finally be where he wanted it to be.

He had no doubt whatsoever that his mother had caved. She'd never stood up to anyone in her entire life.

* * * *

"Do you know what I would like to do?" Lily grinned when Ryan chuckled. "No, Ryan, not that. At least not just this minute."

"Sorry. What is it you would like to do…other than make love to me again?"

"We can't make love in this hammock." Lily had finally gotten used to the sense of being suspended above the ground, and to the swaying. She was pretty sure the ropes wouldn't give way suddenly and dump her on the grass. But she didn't think the contraption could be trusted to hold while they had sex.

"Now you've challenged me, and very shortly I'll have to prove you wrong. What is it you want to do, sweetheart?"

"I want to travel."

"Traveling is good."

Lily snuggled into him, her heart melting when he gathered her closer. How had she survived all these years without being held? Now that she knew what it felt like to be in Ryan's arms, now that she'd tasted the warmth and the security of being held, she wanted never to do without it.

Reg had never held her. Even when they first married, his displays of affection had been few and far between. One kiss before copulation and one kiss after. But an afternoon spent simply snuggling? It never happened.

"Is there any place in particular you want to go?"

His question brought her back to the present, and she stroked Ryan's chest as she thought. She laughed lightly. "Well, I know a few places where I *don't* want to go."

"And that would be?"

"A handful of cities where Reg traveled over the years for conferences. He never took me along, but I'm quite certain he didn't go to them alone."

"Any of those cities in Australia?"

"No. All of them are in North America. Australia?"

"Yeah. I'd like to see Australia. That would be a long trip, though. You'd want to stay for at least a month. And I'd like to go back to England and Scotland. I walked the grounds of Stirling Castle and could have sworn I heard the sounds of battle, the ring of claymores as they clashed, and the scream of men as they died. It gave me shivers. I'd like to share those things with you Lily, see them again through your eyes."

"You'd like to travel with me?" Lily winced at the tone. She'd sounded almost pathetically hopeful. In the next instant, she found herself no longer cuddled next to Ryan, but on top of him.

"I want to spend the rest of my life with you, Lily. But I'm not going to ask for that commitment right now. You need to see more and do more and feel more. You deserve to live, to put yourself first. When we've traveled, when we've seen and done and felt, then I'll ask. I'll ask you for forever. But for now, this is enough."

How could he know her so well? How could he understand the mass of conflicting emotions that streamed through her veins? She wanted him. Oh, she wanted him with a passion so fierce it amazed her continually that it didn't set fire to them both, consume them both completely. But she had other emotions inside her, emotions that had only recently been set free and needed to run their course.

Anger ran so deep within her, Lily felt ashamed to call it her own. This anger had been there all along, beneath the cloak of her indifference, simmering and waiting for its moment to erupt. It had been born out of the pain and emptiness growing where her mother's love should have been, and then fed by years of emotional abuse from her husband. She could not consider herself blameless in the creation of this anger, for she understood the failure to connect properly with her own children was *her* failure. In some ways, she'd been a good mother to her babies. She had fed and nurtured, hugged and loved. But she'd fallen down in the discipline, in that part of parenting that required her to guide her children to become responsible adults. In this, Ryan had spoken the truth.

Her eyes had been opened now, and she had much to settle, within herself and without, before she could freely join her life, forever, to another's. So, no, he couldn't ask her yet, nor could she answer. But she could offer him one very important thing.

"I love you."

* * * *

Ryan smiled, the words never failing to heat his blood and trip his heart.

"I love you, too."

He brought her head down and feasted on her mouth. Hers was an exotic flavor. Addicted, he wanted never to go without the taste of her. He loved the way she responded, the way she melted into him, squirmed to get closer. So damn open and giving, he thought her a wonder.

"Lift up." He could tell by the look of surprise on her face she hadn't noticed his busy fingers opening her shorts. She lifted her hips and he slid the garment down, and off—and at the same time opened his own pants.

"I'm not taking my panties off."

Ryan chuckled at the prim challenge. He caressed her nylon-covered bottom, pushing her against the hard ridge of his engorged cock.

"No, huh? So, you don't want to feel my cock inside you?"

"I didn't say that."

Ryan pulled her down so that he could drink from her lips once more. Restless hands smoothed over her ass and moved her against him. He felt the hard peaks of her nipples poking him through both their shirts. She wore no bra, but he'd gone one better.

"Oh, my."

"Yep. I picked a good day to go commando, didn't I?"

His hungry cock, unfettered by underwear, had worked its way past the thin barrier of the nylon crotch and pulsed slow and deep within the folds of her pussy.

"Move on me, baby, tiny little movements. Get us both wet."

"Ryan, you drive me crazy."

"Do I? That's nothing compared with what you do to me." He took over the motion, his smile almost feral. He felt her resistance, and met her laughing eyes. She teased him, the little minx, teased them both.

"Fuck!" he lifted her, whipped the nylon from her, then brought her hips back down. As soon as he felt her flesh on his, he used his hands to push her into a sitting position, then burrowed them under her shirt to squeeze her breasts.

"Grab the condom out of my right pocket and slip it on me, would you please? My hands are busy at the moment."

"Do you always go around with condoms in your pockets?"

"Only since taking up with you, darling."

He nearly laughed at the look of concentration on her face, and the way she seemed to be moving ever so carefully. Likely, she was afraid she'd tip them over. He hissed softly when she took his penis in her hands and covered him with the latex.

"Now, take me inside you, baby. Fuck me."

Hot and wet, tight and terrific, he felt nearly drowned in the sensations as she raised herself up, then settled on him again. Her sheath swallowed his cock, until he could feel the lips of her pussy caressing his groin. Their movements slow and gentle, the hammock that supported them rocked in an easy, light rhythm.

He loved watching Lily's face when she became lost in the moment, when she got so close to coming that her entire body tensed and strived. That look came upon her now. Reaching down, he used his fingers to stroke her clit, then gritted his teeth to hold back his own orgasm when hers flooded over him.

"I love you, Lily." He brought her down so their lips could touch, their tongues dance as he let go. Her pussy still shivered in delight, and his penis reveled in it, and in her. As she collapsed on him, he enveloped her in his arms holding her tight. Just holding her.

* * * *

A ham baked in the oven, and the scent of it filled the house. Lily wasn't certain how many diner guests she would have. Ryan would be there, of course. She'd invited her son and daughter, and her ex-husband and his wife. She'd also extended the invitation to her mother, though that woman had not said if she would attend, or not. She'd included one other person whom she knew without a doubt would be there. She had a nice zinfandel chilling, an amazing peach cobbler cooling, and a definite agenda simmering.

"Are you sure about this, sweetheart?"

Lily knew that Ryan's heart was in the right place, and that he worried on her behalf. She went over, hugged him tight, and kissed him soundly.

"Yes, I'm sure. A lot of what John said was pure crap. But he and Alice *are* my children, and I do feel an obligation to assist them with their educational expenses."

"I know you do. I also know that you'd like to build better relationships with the both of them. I just don't want you to be too disappointed if things don't work out that way. You can only go halfway, darling. They have to come the rest of the way themselves."

"I know. And I also know that my mother is likely never going to change. I…I can't have her interfering in my life anymore, as she's always done. It breaks my heart to say this, but I may have to cut all ties to her. And that would be like history repeating itself, because I know she did the same thing when she left home, before she met and married my father."

At his questioning look, she walked into the living room, and opened the middle drawer of her newly refurbished desk. She handed him the book she kept there.

"Your mother's diary?" he asked after opening it.

"Yes. Anger and bitterness seethed in every word, and I couldn't understand it. How could a twelve-year-old girl have such darkness inside her for her own parents? Then I found this section." She took the book, and opened it to where she wanted him to read.

When he looked up at her again, she read his expression. "No, it doesn't excuse her behavior. But it does go some ways in explaining it."

"Lots of kids are adopted, Lily."

"Yes. But not many are the illegitimate child of an heiress."

Chapter 18

"How much do you know of the story?"

"Quite a bit, now. I guess Uncle Mark must have figured it out when he went through all the old family documents, not long before he died. He left them for me to easily find, packed in new cartons, in plain sight right at the top of the attic stairs."

Lily smiled as Ryan simply began to set the table for her as she continued to prepare the dinner. In the time she'd known him, he'd cooked dinner, ran the washer and dryer, and had even vacuumed her living room. How nice to be with a man who simply shared the duties of day-to-day living.

Because she wanted to share, too, she began to tell him what she knew. "Apparently, during the 1930s, my grandparents had as much trouble as everyone else making ends meet. Uncle Mark, just a boy himself, helped my grandfather with the farm, of course, but it wasn't enough. My grandmother, through friends, found work in Toronto, with a wealthy family. The Westerlys hired my grandmother as a housekeeper—sort of like head of the household staff. Tough for her to be away from her husband and son for weeks at a time, but the era was known for people having to do hard things. Anyway, the Westerly's had a son, Chad, and a daughter, Amelia. I think the daughter was only fifteen when my grandmother went to work there in nineteen thirty-eight. A romance brewed between Amelia and one of the staff—my grandmother doesn't say who, in her own journal, only that the man had been hired for a time, then left. Amelia became pregnant. The family freaked. A common reaction in those days. They made arrangements for Amelia to be sent away until she had the baby. I guess because Mrs. Westerly trusted my grandmother, and because my grandmother couldn't have any more children, they paid to have Amelia kept here for the duration of her pregnancy. They had homes for unwed mothers in those days, of course, but from what I've read of the letters Mrs. Westerly sent to my grandmother, she feared her daughter's situation would become known if she went to one of them. The farm suited her purposes, being far enough away from the city so that no one in the family's social circle would know, and isolated enough that the secret could be kept. When the baby arrived, my grandparents adopted her."

"How did your mother find out?"

Lily replaced the lid on the pot of potatoes, then turned and leaned against the stove. "My grandmother told her she was adopted, though she didn't reveal the identity of her birth mother. On her own, my mother searched out the details—my grandmother had kept the letters from Mrs. Westerly, and she found them."

"So your mother figures that if she hadn't been adopted by your grandmother—she would have grown up rich?" Ryan had just set the last of the glasses on the table, and looked up at her.

"I think that's exactly what she thought at the time. I know that when she left here, she never returned. My dad brought me out to visit my uncle and grandparents. But Dad never told me why mother never came with us."

"Does knowing your mother's history help?"

"Yes, it does. Because I can at least *understand* why she is as she is."

"Whatever became of the Westerlys?" He leaned back against the counter and folded his arms, mimicking Lily's pose.

"From what I understand, Amelia married a doctor and moved to British Columbia. Her father didn't do such a good job preserving the family fortune as his predecessors had done. He died in the early seventies, and there wasn't much left of the estate."

"Does your mother know that?"

"I have no idea." She turned around to adjust the oven temperature, then walked over to Ryan. "Like I said, at least now I understand where her anger and bitterness has come from. And I understand why she took to Reg right away and favored him over me."

"Because he represents the social sphere she believes she belongs in?"

"Exactly. She married my father, I'm guessing because she chose to, but she was never really happy with him. I don't think he ever made enough money to suit her, though I think he did pretty well. I guess her real problem is that she's stuck in a nineteen fifties mindset. Upper class, in my opinion, has nothing to do with money, and everything to do with the inner person."

"Amen to that." He stood back, surveyed the table. "Well, I guess we're ready here."

Lily chuckled. "Yeah. The only thing left to say is, send in the clowns."

* * * *

"Pass the ham, please." Ryan's wink accompanied his request, and was returned by Lily's smile. Any other woman would have crumbled under the strain by now.

When he'd arrived, Reg had sent a scathing glance toward the set table, then shot Lily a disapproving look. "I thought we were invited here to discuss sensitive family business."

Reg's emphasis on the word 'family,' deliberately aimed at Ryan, made him chuckle. "Ouch, I guess that tells me," he'd replied as he went over to Lily and slipped his arm around her waist.

"That's strange. Because *I* always thought a dinner invitation implied the sharing of a meal." When her ex looked like he would protest further, Lily opened her hands graciously, inviting all to sit. "We will discuss business. After we eat."

"I hope your wife is well," the short brunette Lily had introduced as Pam asked of Reg.

"Quite well, thank you. I couldn't see any reason to include her in this...gathering."

Ryan caught Lily's expression then and did his best not to laugh. Apparently, including a wife in anything wasn't something Reginald Martin could find reason for, ever. He admired his lady's restraint in not pointing that out.

In short order, dinner guests had been seated, wine poured, and food served.

"Alice, I never did ask you last week. Are you still planning to go back to U of T in the fall?"

"Yeah. I'm entering the final year of my undergrad degree in English. Once I get that, I'm not completely sure what it is I want to do. I thought I might teach."

"Oh, now that would be interesting. Alice, a teacher."

Her brother's snide tone stiffened Alice's back. Ryan wondered how the little monster continually got away with acting like an asshole.

"It is interesting," Lily immediately agreed, flashing her daughter a smile. "I think Alice would make a wonderful teacher."

"You do?"

Lily must have also heard the self-doubt in Alice's voice, for she immediately nodded. "I do. You have excellent people skills, and a way with kids. I noticed that when you served as camp counselor. If that's what would make you happy, I say go for it. What age group?"

"Elementary grades. Maybe even junior high."

"Well, your brother has certainly provided you with ample experience dealing with the pre-adolescent attitude."

"I beg your pardon?" John gave his mother a look that mimicked his father's.

"And so you should," his mother replied quietly. "Immature and rude behavior is never appropriate, and always requires an apology."

The look of shock John wore was priceless. Ryan would have laughed, but he knew how hard it had been for Lily to say what needed to be said. The look of surprise on Alice's face made him realize that she had likely suffered the same treatment, at least from her brother, as had her mother.

"I don't have to stay here and be treated like this."

"You do if you want any financial assistance from me." Lily looked right at him then, and Ryan wanted to cheer when John finally gave way and lowered his eyes.

"I think it may be time to get to the heart of this evening's entertainment," she said then, challenging her ex with just a look. When her attention switched to Ryan, he gave her a nod of encouragement. Getting to his feet, he placed a hand on Lily's shoulder. "I'll clear the dishes, put on the coffee. If you'd like to take everyone into the living room?"

* * * *

It amazed Lily that things had gone as well as they had so far. She waited for Ryan to join them, then nodded to Pam, who had brought her briefcase into the room with her. Lily alone remained standing, and as Pam began to speak Lily braced her back against the window, her attention riveted on her family.

"Mr. Martin, I have here sworn affidavits from Lily's own doctor, from a psychiatrist in private practice, and from her investment broker. They all essentially say the same thing. My client—Lily Martin—is sane, competent, and quite capable of managing her own affairs. Should anyone be thinking of trying to prove otherwise, it would be practically impossible to do so. It is most difficult to have an adult declared incompetent in this province even *with* sufficient cause and evidence. In this case, there would be no chance of that happening, whatsoever."

Lily watched as the expressions chased across Reg's face. When she had thought ahead to this moment, she imagined she might feel powerful. But all she really felt was relief. Reginald Martin no longer had any power over her. She had taken it back after years of marriage. Now, noting the basically shocked and surprised look on his face, she couldn't help but chuckle.

"You shouldn't be surprised. It wasn't difficult to figure out what you and my mother had in mind."

"Your mother is quite convinced that you're…sick. As she is the woman who raised you, I bowed to her greater knowledge of you."

That was a slap, and a part of Lily wanted to respond in kind. Instead, she made her tone dismissive. "I'll deal with my mother later."

She took a moment to look at the faces of her children. John's expression mirrored his father's. But Alice...Alice's lips turned up in a slight smile. That simple fact gave her hope. They had begun to build a tentative relationship over just one lunch. Lily really wanted to share the kind of loving relationship with her daughter that had been denied to her. Refocusing on the present, she looked to Ryan, nodded in response to his wink, and turned her attention to her children.

"It is time that I did something in order to help pay for your educations. John was right in that. But he was quite wrong to think that he could somehow manipulate me into selling my home.

"If I did sell this place, I would be under no obligation whatsoever to share the proceeds of that sale with anyone. You're both legally adults, legally responsible for your own lives. But I've not done much to help you financially—or to help you become responsible adults. All that is about to change."

Lily nodded to Pam, who drew two folders out of her briefcase. She handed one to each of Lily's children.

"These are contracts. Once signed, they will be legally binding. I'll let you read them over, but essentially what they say is that if you are willing to get jobs and contribute to your educations, then I will contribute, too. These contracts are very clear. For every one hundred dollars you earn, I'll kick in three. I'll provide money to assist you in getting apartments, if that's what you choose to do. I'll give you, outright, the first and last month's rent, and will subsidize—not pay in full, but subsidize—your rent to a maximum of three hundred dollars a month. I will also cover the full cost of your text books and will contribute twenty per cent of the cost of your tuitions. Now, this will allow your father to cut back on some of the educational obligations he's been underwriting, but not all of them. Take a few days to look over the contracts. But bear in mind, this is the only offer that I am going to make. Should you turn it down, you are on your own, financially, as far as I am concerned."

John jumped to his feet, barely letting her finish. "This is bullshit! Who the fuck do you think you are, trying to tell me what to do and trying to run my life this way—a job, for God's sake! Well, I won't stand for it! You can't treat me like this! And if Grandmother knew—"

"If your grandmother knew, John, it would change nothing. The time is done when you can use her to threaten me, or use her to get your way with me. Don't you think it's time for you to grow up? Become a man?"

"Go to hell."

The sound of the door slamming echoed through the room. Lily turned her eyes to her ex and saw, with some surprise, his embarrassment. Alice sighed, breaking the silence.

"He's just mad. When he cools down, he'll realize that this is a pretty good deal, Mom."

"Is it?"

"Yeah, it is. I have no problem with getting a job. I didn't really bother before because the only ones I could get paid minimum wage, for part time hours—and it was easy to just let Dad pay for everything. But this is a good deal."

Lily thought she would cry when her daughter hugged her. "I want us to spend more time together," she said quietly.

"Me too. I'm proud of you, Mom. I never said that before."

Lily stroked a hand down Alice's hair. "I've never given you much of a reason to be proud of me before."

Reginald got to his feet. "I'll speak to John. I'll tell him the only way he will get his tuition paid by me is if he accepts your offer. It is a generous one."

"He wants us out of the house, and to be honest, I want out, too," Alice said after her father left. "I'll speak to John too, Mom."

* * * *

"Congratulations. You handled them all beautifully," Ryan said when, a few minutes later, all their guests had left.

"Well," Lily replied as she turned into his arms. "Not all of them. There's one more to go."

"Baby, you don't have to. You could just...leave things as they are. Wait for her to contact you. Chances are, she'll act as if nothing has happened."

"Six months ago...hell, six weeks ago, that's what I would have done. But I'm not hiding behind a shield of acquiescence anymore. I think the time has come for me to beard the lioness in her den."

"I'm worried, because I have a feeling she's going to use her claws and rake the hell out of you."

"Then I'll be expecting you to stand by with the first aid kit."

Chapter 19

Lily felt as if she had come full circle.

The home on North Shore Boulevard showed signs of age. When built in the nineteen fifties, it had been a show place, a grand house in the grandest neighborhood of the city of Burlington. As Lily got out of her car, she noted that the paint needed refreshing, and the roof replacing.

She'd never spent much time thinking about how her mother managed, financially speaking. Eloise Robertson Riggs always seemed to be in control of everything, and everyone around her. But now, looking at this old house through fresh eyes, she wondered.

All her life, Lily had wanted her mother to love her. She'd always been grateful, of course, for the nice clothes and all the extras—music and dance lessons, vacations, and spending money. She had been the only one in her senior class to drive a brand new car. But even as a teen, she thought she could have done without some of those frills if it meant having a mother whom she knew loved her.

Instead, it had always seemed as if her mother had—maybe not *hated* her so much as *resented* her. And she'd never known why.

Now that she understood her mother's core bitterness, she thought she could figure out the why. But she was tired of speculating, and tired of letting everything her mother did, or didn't do, eat away at her.

Lily didn't knock. She'd never knocked on this door. In years past, when her father had been alive, they had employed a housekeeper three days a week. As Lily closed the door behind her, she realized there'd been no housekeeper here for nearly five years. Yet the interior of the home had been kept ruthlessly spotless. In fact, it didn't really look as if anyone actually *lived* here. The room not only lacked clutter, it lacked character. No photographs graced tables or mantles, not a single personal touch warmed the space.

Just shy of nine in the morning, Lily knew her mother would be in the kitchen, having her second cup of tea and reading the newspaper. She smiled, slightly, when she entered the back room and saw her doing just that.

"Good morning, Mother."

"I should think you'd be ashamed to show your face, considering your behavior over the last few weeks. Cavorting with outlaw bikers, threatening your own children, being rude to Reginald."

Lily grabbed a cup from the cupboard, and poured herself a cup of tea. Why had she always felt so jittery here? Why had that tone of voice from her mother always chilled her blood and frozen her spirit? She smiled as she realized not only did she not *feel* any of those things, she actually thought her mother was—well, kind of funny.

"You forgot to add terrorizing a hapless realtor and running off a Children's Aid worker."

"Don't you sass me, young lady! I raised you better than that."

"Did you? Hmm." Lily set her cup down. "All right, let's get to it, shall we? Ryan Kincaid, the man I am in love with, does ride a motorcycle. He is not, however, a member of any biker gang, outlaw or otherwise. I did not threaten my children. I challenged them. Not that they *are* children, just acting like them from time to time, no thanks to you. As for Reginald—well, he's a big boy and can take care of himself."

Then she set her tea down, not even irritated that her mother appeared to be reading the paper and ignoring her.

"I know you were adopted, Mother. I found your diary, and Grandmother's journal. I know about your birth family. I realize that must have been very upsetting for you, to learn that. And to think—"

"You know nothing! Nothing!"

Oh, she had her mother's attention now, all right. Eloise had thrown down the paper and surged to her feet.

"I had to live with dirt farmers! *Dirt farmers,* as if I had been just a common whore's cast-off mistake. I deserved better things than growing up poor. My birthright should have been a mansion in Rosedale, not a dilapidated shack out in the sticks! If that woman hadn't been so desperate for a child, for a daughter, my life would have been one of status and privilege!"

Shocked at the depth of her mother's bitterness, Lily couldn't speak for a long moment. She watched as her mother turned her back, looked out the window toward the lake.

"I went there. To that house on Bayview Avenue. When I finally put that farm behind me, I went to my family. *My real family.* They denied me. A picture hung over the mantel, a picture of my mother. *My real mother.* And she looked just like me. But they said it wasn't true. "You're no relation of ours," they said. And I knew who to blame. She took me, and it was *her* fault they didn't want me anymore."

In those words, Lily heard the pain of a disillusioned child. All the hurt she herself had felt all these years paled in comparison.

"You have to know that's not true. Nowadays, single women have children, and there's no taint, no scandal. But in those days, Mother, for a young woman to get pregnant outside of marriage—especially for a young woman of society to do so—meant a terrible scandal. The Westerlys never would have kept you. Never. And it had nothing at all to do with *you,* and everything to do with their own priorities. If Grandmother hadn't adopted you, either someone else would have, or most likely, you would have been placed in an orphanage. You would have grown up bearing the label 'illegitimate.' That's just the way things happened in those days. You have to know that's the truth."

Her mother didn't say a word, but the sound of her ragged breathing said it all. Lily knew she listened, but had no idea if her words would make any difference.

"You married my father. He gave you a good life."

Her mother whirled around, her face and tone filled with contempt. "He was a foolish man, content to be Vice President of his uncle's company. He could have been President. He could have worked harder—worked smarter. But he wanted to be a *family man*, not a company man. He thought spending time with you more important than raising our status in the community."

Lily felt as if her heart would pound out of her chest. Epiphanies, she thought almost absently, were funny things. She'd experienced a few in her life, and always before they had been during quiet moments of introspection and reflection. This was the first time she'd had one in the middle of an emotional confrontation with her mother. She'd come here this morning, she realized suddenly, still hoping for an apology, some words from her mother that would heal old wounds. And that, she understood at last, wasn't going to happen. Not now, and likely, not ever. Only *she* could perform the magic of healing her own wounds.

As a sense of peace descended on her, she turned her attention back to her mother. "He was right. Mother...I don't know what to say to you. For as long as I can remember, you have accused me, over and over, of being selfish, and of blaming everyone else for my own failings. And now I finally see the truth. That's not me. It has never been me. It's you."

"How dare you!"

Her mother's contempt had morphed to fury. Lily couldn't stop now. "Oh, I dare. Not to hurt you, Mother. Despite everything, I don't want to hurt you. But the truth is, it's *you* who've been selfish, seeing only what you wanted for yourself out of life, never looking to the needs of your husband, or your child. Spurning and hurting your parents and your brother, because they'd dared to love you. You blame your unhappiness on Grandmother, for adopting you, on Father for not being rich enough. But your unhappiness is only your fault. I feel so sorry for you. Because you could have chosen to be happy, if you had wanted to. All those years spent in bitterness and anger, when they could have been years overflowing with blessings and joy. Nobody else's fault, Mother, and no one to blame, but yourself."

* * * *

"You look good."

"I feel good."

He'd been a little worried that morning when Lily had kissed him goodbye and headed off on her own to see her mother. He didn't care if waiting for her right here in her driveway showed how worried he had been. But looking at her now, he could see a lightness of spirit that hadn't been there just a few hours before.

"So…what happened?" When she began to walk toward the grassy backyard and the pool, he walked beside her.

"I let it go. It was never my mother who had to change. Well—she does, but only if she wants to be happy, and a part of my family. *I* had to change. I had to accept that she is as she is, and that how she behaved all those years had nothing to do with me. And I had to forgive her, and let it go."

Ryan looked at her for a long moment, his heart so full of love and pride that he couldn't speak at first. Finally, he managed, "You're one hell of a woman, Lily Martin."

"Yes, I am, aren't I?"

When she turned to him, he opened his arms, snuggled her close. "I love you, Lily."

"Your love is my miracle."

Ryan felt his face coloring, and in sheer defense, swooped in and stole a kiss. "You're going to make me blush."

"I *am* making you blush. But it's the truth. Before you rode into my life on that monster Harley, I was a self-involved wimp. I had no spine, no goals, and no self-respect. You took off your helmet and took me off guard. You helped me find my feminine power. And because you did, because you loved me, everything changed for me. That's what you are to me. Everything."

"There's that word again."

Ryan loved Lily's laughter. He loved it even more when she rose up and touched her lips to his. Her kiss, warm and a little timid, intoxicated him. He took the kiss deeper, his arms holding her close, his hands roaming her back, hungry to touch her.

"No. This time let me. Let me show you," she whispered the plea breathlessly. Ryan submitted.

Women had undressed him before, but never with the reverence Lily put in her touch. Each button opened revealed more flesh that she kissed and caressed. The tenderness, the love she poured over him nearly brought him to his knees. Her nails scraped lightly over his nipples and he shivered. His penis hardened in response to the promise of her lips, tongue, and hands. His shirt fell to the grass, and hers followed, cast off with an impatient gesture. She ditched her bra and then rubbed those wonderful breasts of hers against his chest.

"Darling...we're outside and it's the middle of the morning," he felt compelled to remind her. All the other times he'd taken her outside, she'd been careful to be discreet, just in case. She showed no discretion this time. They stood, unsheltered, for all to see.

"I don't care. I'm having you, here and now."

* * * *

Lily didn't care that they stood outside in broad daylight. She didn't care if anyone saw them, or not. She needed to show this wonderful man how much she loved him, how much she loved making love with him.

His chest and shoulders and arms, muscled and strong, never failed to entice her. She felt powerful that she could make him shiver, that her mouth on his nipple, the nip of her teeth could weaken him. Needing more than anything to give, she opened his pants and dropped to her knees.

His cock was magnificent, hard, quivering at the touch of her hand. She craved the essence of him. In this act of love, he had been the first, and she rejoiced in the sheer joy of that. She'd become addicted so quickly to the taste of him, so that when she took him into her mouth, her arousal climbed, every part of her melted in pleasure. The feel of his hands in her hair as he bent into her, as he accepted her gift, thrilled her. And when she had driven him to lose control, when he pushed her onto the grass, shoved her skirt and panties out of the way and plunged into her, she knew her power to be complete.

His mouth plundered hers, and she gave, rising up, reversing their positions. With impatient hands, she pulled off the rest of her clothes, and straddled him, initiating a slow, delicious ride. She arched her back, arms spread out. She couldn't hold back, couldn't stop the waves of orgasm from overwhelming her, and her hands, reaching skyward, grasped at air, proclaiming her victory. Never again would she feel inadequate, never again would she doubt herself, or her appeal.

She was woman, powerful, complete. She had bloomed.

Epilogue

Fifteen months later

On the breeze she could smell something rich and fragrant, as if someone had sprayed a cloud of perfume nearby. The hum of voices seemed a blur in the distance, and with her eyes closed, floating in that half-asleep state, an anchor to reality. Over and above and around everything else, the constant pulse of the ocean lulled and soothed.

This, Lily's first trip to the Caribbean, wouldn't be her last. Movement beside her had her turning her head. Firm masculine lips met hers, and Lily lost herself in the kiss.

"Miss me?"

Lily smiled. She didn't think he'd been gone from the chaise next to hers for more than a few minutes. Affecting a blasé tone, she said, "Oh, did you go somewhere?"

"Smart ass."

"I am. Where *did* you go, by the way?" She asked the question, but had a sneaking suspicion she knew where he had been and what he had been doing.

"Just went back to the room for a moment. Wanted to see if we had any phone messages."

Lily opened her eyes, and sat up in the chaise. Picking up the fresh piña colada Ryan had brought her, she took a long, appreciative sip. Directly in front of her just off the coast, a catamaran raced with the wind. They'd taken a sail on one the day before. Another first for her that belonged to the man beside her. To the left, the resort's enormous pool beckoned her. Her bathing suit had dried. Time to get it wet again.

"I'm sure everything is fine back home. I never knew you could be such a worrier."

"How much do we know about this guy that Alice is moving in with? Not very much. Okay, they've been dating for nearly a year, but still. I don't like him."

"You liked him fine last month."

"Last month, they weren't living together."

"He's a good guy, Ryan. You know it. I know it. Besides, you know Sheila and John will keep an eye out. But Alice is old enough to make her own choices."

"I know. It's good that Alice and Sheila are so close. Gives me some peace of mind. That Sheila's got a damn good head on her shoulders."

Lily's life was full.

She volunteered with the Literacy Council and spent a couple of evenings a week helping to teach adults to read. Encouraged by Ryan, she had also enrolled in some university courses. She had a love of history, and though she felt no burning need to pursue a degree, the courses she took fascinated her. Afraid she'd be the oldest person in her class, Lily discovered one of her classmates was a seventy-five-year-old grandmother with ten grandchildren. She'd also begun touring yard sales and flea markets, looking for pieces of furniture she could make over. One piece, a beautiful cherry coffee table, now sat in her living room along with the secretary desk.

But Lily's greatest pleasure—aside from her relationship with Ryan— had become her relationships with her children.

John had finally come around, and accepted Lily's challenge. When he'd been working part time for two months and moved into his own apartment, he'd begun seeing Sheila again.

Lily's relationship with both her children had improved dramatically over the last year. That relationship had expanded to include Ryan. Interesting, she mused, how protective he'd become of Alice, and how supportive he was of John. Ryan proved a good influence on her son.

Several times, she'd seen the two of them alone together, in deep conversation.

If any sadness clouded her life, it was that her mother had not yet softened her attitude. Lily called the woman at least once a month, keeping the lines of communication open. Those conversations, stilted and difficult, challenged Lily's optimism. But with her grandchildren, Eloise remained more open and receptive.

Lily had come to accept the painful truth that she and her mother would likely never be close. But she knew she'd done all she could in that regard, and felt no guilt.

"The phone bills are going to be really expensive if you do this next year when we're in Australia."

She smiled when Ryan chuckled and lay back against the chaise. When he took her hand in his, their fingers laced.

"Well, that will be next year. Maybe by then, she'll have tired of him, and he'll be history."

"Maybe she'll be pregnant."

"Don't say that!"

Lily laughed, and squeezed Ryan's hand when he sighed. "Yeah, I admit it. I never thought that I'd be so...protective, either."

"I think it's sweet."

"You do?"

"Yes, I do."

"You know what I think would be sweet?"

"No, what?"

"If our trip to Australia in January doubled as our honeymoon. Why don't we get married, sweetheart?"

Lily's gaze locked with his. The love she saw for her in his eyes filled her heart and heated her blood.

"Yeah," Lily replied, her heart overflowing, "Why don't we?"

LILY IN BLOOM

THE END

AUTHOR'S BIO

Morgan has been a writer since she was first able to pick up a pen. In the beginning, it was a hobby, a way to create a world of her own, and who could resist that? Then as she grew, life got in the way, as life often does. She got married and had children, and worked in the field of accounting, for that was the practical thing to do. And all the time she was being practical, she would squirrel herself away on quiet Sunday afternoons and write.

Most children are raised knowing the Ten Commandments and the Golden Rule. Morgan's children also learned the Paper Rule: thou shalt not throw out any paper that hast thy mother's words upon it.

Believing in tradition, Morgan ensured that her children's children learned this rule, too.

Life threw Morgan a curve when, in 2002, she underwent emergency triple by-pass surgery. Second chances are to be cherished, and Morgan decided to use hers to do what she'd always dreamed of doing: writing full time.

Morgan has always loved writing romance. When asked why, she says, "I can't help it. I've lived, I've loved, I've laughed, I've cried. And, I took notes!"

Morgan lives with a cat that has an attitude, a dog that has no dignity, and her husband of thirty-four years.

Come by and visit Morgan at **www.morganashbury.com**.

Siren Publishing, Inc.
www.SirenPublishing.com

LaVergne, TN USA
08 February 2010
172460LV00005B/72/P